Jeremy Chikalto and the Demon Trace

T.S. DEBROSSE

Published by
Viral Cat Press
San Francisco, CA

ISBN: 0692230629

ISBN-13: 978-0692230626

Library of Congress Control Number: 2014910415

Viral Cat Press, San Francisco, CA

"Our two souls therefore, which are one,
Though I must go, endure not yet
A breach, but an expansion,
Like gold to airy thinness beat."

– JOHN DONNE, "A VALEDICTION: FORBIDDING MOURNING"

This book is dedicated to Mirabelle and Faline.

Acknowledgements

I would like to once again give thanks to my family, friends, and loved ones for their continued support. Thanks especially to my husband and editor, J.D. Marshall, for his part in our brainstorming sessions, which almost always ended in laughter. The Hazy Souls series was written long ago when I was a child. I had the plot committed to my heart, and though it's (I'd like the think) a bit more sophisticated now, the initial feelings remain the same. I am in love with my characters—the good, the bad, and everyone in between, and it is a dream come true to have them live on in readers' minds. I feel so blessed to have been able to share Jeremy and Maren's story. Thank you!

CHAPTER 1
ENDURANCE

In the green lands of Watico, a darkness spread from the east. Between the vast falls of the River Elmer and the dreary fenland beyond the mountains, a whisper was heard in the shadows. It called for the young Cajjez. The shadows soon took shape and these were called demons. Anyone who looked into their faces fell back in horror and fled. Some were eaten on the spot, inhaled whole and burned in fiery innards.

It was early afternoon and the sun was hiding behind thin clouds. Wantoro ran along the runway on the roof of the Watican Castle towards a massive spaceship, pushing Raaychila's wheelchair forward at breakneck speed, Mateo snuffling and clearing his throat as he jogged in the rear. Ronny, the royal family's trusted Chief Security Guard, beckoned them from the ramp, "Come on! Hurry up!" The wind and smoke beat them back, but they pressed forward and up the ramp, into safety.

Mateo summoned the track-star days of his youth, and long-jumped through the craft's boarding doors just before they shut. The engines roared and the doors sealed shut as an angry mob made its way to the roof deck. "Death to the Vor!" they shouted.

Wantoro pressed his back into his seat. "Veil this ship."

The spaceship shook slightly as a hologram camouflaged its exterior.

A news broadcaster appeared in front of the gate to the Watican Castle, the air around her flickering in the heat of the flames; to her left, a fallen statue of Vordin Chikalto, founder of the Farmoore Galaxy, lay toppled over:

> "After an intelligence leak following the emergence of demons on Watico, classified government reports of demon sitings are now being disseminated by a group who call themselves 'Leveled Ground.' The group claims that the royal family has been aware of the presence of demons for some time. The demon reports were initially ordered by Cajjez Jeremy Chikalto. We're receiving word on the roof of the eastern side of the castle that Vor Wantoro has fled the area in a spacecraft. Meanwhile in Bilencia, what appears to be a mass assault by an unknown species has struck the village of Hagden, taking with it forty-nine civilians. Some witnesses have survived and video footage has been confiscated. Missing persons reports are expected to rise dramatically. If anyone has any information on the whereabouts of Cajjez Jeremy Chikalto or the royal family, you are urged to contact your local military order or to call your county representative."

The spacecraft was now in the dark of space. Wantoro nodded to Ronny and he turned off the news. "Jeremy and Maren will go into hiding."

* * *

"Master Apollyon, we will serve thee."

Jeremy, Maren, Tina, and Lyrna were huddled in a cavern in the center of the Earth, in a madhouse known as Mantel's Maze, and now they were being rescued by demons. It was dark and cold, and they were surrounded by gray stone walls on all sides, except a little torchlight filtered in from a neighboring room where the wall had been blasted open from battle.

As a child, Jeremy's servants brought out the worst in him. In their cowering obedience, they were like so many wounded dogs—and Jeremy loved dogs—but these dogs were whining, always expecting the next blow, which was both an invitation and a self-fulfilling prophesy.

And here, the demons were serving him. But they had always been with him, lurking in the space between him and his subjects, whispering terrible suggestions, shadows looming over his sadism. Was he a puppet all those times? Was the lash he used to inflict pain really a string moving his hand? Or no, were the suggestions his alone, and the demons mere yes-men, flocking to his darkness?

Red eyes glowed in the shadows, like stars in Hell.

"If I'm your Master, then cower before me!" yelled Jeremy, and the demons skittered back to the corners of the room. Jeremy shivered in fear and excitement at his power.

Maren shook her head in disbelief and Tina lay crumpled on the floor.

"Christ, I need to get out of here." Jeremy panted and wiped his hand across his mouth, perspiring fiercely. "I'm burning up. I have a fever," he whimpered. The debris and blood from the battle cluttered the rock floor; a piece of Mantel's cloak lay torn and burnt inches from Jeremy's foot.

"She's breathing." Maren nudged Jeremy forward.

He bent down over Tina and placed his head on her chest. "We'll give her some time to recover, and then we'll...?"

Maren kept an eye on the demons and leaned forward towards Jeremy. "We'll go," she finished his sentence. "It's good that they listen to you—"

"That's not good."

"For the sake of survival." Maren straightened. "Just keep them away. Make sure they understand."

Jeremy nodded and stood up to face one of his demons. "Rise up."

The demon wavered and hissed.

"Fly up, towards the ceiling!" Jeremy gritted his teeth. "They aren't listening to me."

Maren grabbed his arm. "They speak Latin. You don't know *any* Latin?"

"I'm sorry I wasn't such a fantastic Earth Studies scholar," he said.

"Exsurge, surgo," said Maren. The demons eyed her suspiciously. "You say it," she whispered.

"Exsurge. Surgo." Still the demons didn't move. Jeremy cursed and began pacing the center of the small stone room. "If I could just get them to rise up—!"

Suddenly, the demons rose, some even disappearing in the Haze. Jeremy spun around to Maren. "It worked!" He smiled maniacally.

"What did you do differently?"

Jeremy paused. "I imagined them doing it. The words —Latin, English, Vespian or whatever—don't command them. It's my will." He slumped back onto the floor, suddenly exhausted. He hadn't slept in forty-eight hours.

Maren held up Tina's hand to him. "We need to get her home to New York."

Jeremy frowned and faced his demons, who were hanging out near the ceiling of the cavern swishing forked tails. "Right," he said. "But then I'm taking you back to the Farmoore Galaxy." Jeremy wrapped his arms around Maren and Tina and brought them into the Haze. Lyrna followed. They raced forward through purple clouds. Demons floated around Jeremy on every plane, bowing low as he passed, and the spirit animals shrank back into the purple depths.

New York. Jeremy knew it distinctly from inside the Haze. He could feel the inside of Maren's apartment on Park Avenue, and could feel Ms. Donegall's Estate, the bleary nights of wine, perfume, and dancing. He pulled the party out of the Haze and into the back lot of a convenience store, setting Maren and Tina gently on the pavement. Jeremy had never been to Tina's New York house, but guessed it was close to Maren's. The night air was cool and wet, and it was "dark" in the city, with pink smog illuminated by ambient lighting. Jeremy heard a skittering behind him, and half expected Lyrna to hop on his lap.

Instead, a dog-sized demon that was more or less a cockroach scuttled up to Jeremy, and he shooed it away in disgust. He willed it back into the Haze. Jeremy glanced around to make sure no one saw it. There was a couple leaning on the side of the convenience store, but they were too busy arguing to notice demons. Jeremy frowned at Maren, who had gotten to her feet. "I might slip up. I don't know if I can keep them back."

"You're doing great," said Maren.

"Where does Tina live?" he asked, trying not to think about demons. He'd have to try harder.

"Fifth Avenue." Maren stumbled forward and caught herself on Jeremy's arm. "We have to keep moving. I'm just a little dizzy. We have to get her back."

Tina was laying motionless on the pavement except for a slow breath. Jeremy picked Tina up in a fireman's carry, and began to walk towards Fifth Avenue. She opened her eyes for a spell and Jeremy smiled at her. She slipped back into an uneasy sleep. Some type of festival was going on in Central Park. A passerby gawked at Jeremy's shredded pink button down, the silk fabric caked onto his body in sweat, blood, and ash. He looked like a refugee carrying his friend out of the jungle. Tina's clothes were mostly just soot and Maren fared only slightly better in a torn green tunic.

Jeremy helped Tina to her feet when they reached her front door. She was groggily coming to, and could manage to slump upright against Jeremy's chest. Maren rang the doorbell.

Jeremy leaned in to Tina. "We'll just drop you off, I'm sure the police are looking for me. Not that that matters anymore."

"We'll see you soon," whispered Maren as the door creaked open.

Tina's father, a tall, strong man with a military cut, fell on his daughter with a bear hug. "My little girl!" Caught in the moment, he barely processed Maren and Jeremy. They ducked out to a side alley, just as a light rain began to patter on their heads. The alleyway was roomy and clean, with an organized cluster of trash receptacles at the far side.

"What a well-kept alleyway," said Jeremy, crossing his arms. "She'll be okay. Janet and Greg?"

Maren shook her head. "Tina will tell them I'm all right. Let's just go back home. It's been some trip."

CHAPTER 2

STAY HIDDEN

"Lyrna!" Jeremy pulled Maren through to the Haze and she collapsed in his arms—a weightless passenger in his freak jet. "I wish you could be here with me, Maren," he said. Jeremy glanced around at the undulating waves of purple clouds. The dead passed through like rain drops to some other plane. A camel marched solemnly past him, dragging an old woman along behind it. Then they crossed into some other fold in space.

"Lyrna!" Jeremy slung Maren over his shoulder and swam along. Lyrna was close.

"Mew! Follow." She peeped out of a cloud and twitched her nose at him. Just as he was getting ready to follow her, he felt some demons close in on him from behind.

Soon row after row of demons faced Jeremy, with more filtering in every second.

Jeremy strained not to think about the demons, and raced after Lyrna.

With Lyrna's help, Jeremy ferried Maren through the Haze, pulling out at select planets for oxygen, until at last they arrived on Watico. He pulled Maren through to his bedroom and lay her on his bed. They needed to rest. His demons would remain in the Haze—he'd make sure of it. Jeremy closed his eyes and massaged his temples. *Stay hidden*, he thought, and he set his mind on forging a connection with the dark matter veiled behind the air. Then he felt a snag, or was it a tug—he'd baited his demons and they felt like a menacing vacuum—a soul drain. Jeremy took a deep breath and concentrated on holding his line. An electrical current zapped his brain, then traveled down his spine and exited through his sternum. He could feel that the demons were strong and that they meant to take him, but he held fast and the energy surged through him like a closed circuit. He took a deep breath—and then coughed and lost his connection.

Something was wrong. Jeremy could smell a heavy timber smoldering somewhere—plastic and rubber, too. And something more noxious. Gathering his senses, Jeremy raced forward and reached for the door knob. It felt hot. He flung the door open and smoke billowed in, filling his nostrils and making him cough violently. He slammed the door closed. "Maren, there's a fire!" She tossed and turned in bed, rubbing her eyes.

"Will someone put it out?" she asked dreamily.

Jeremy began pacing his room. "You need oxygen. I'm taking you outside."

"Why is there a fire?"

Jeremy wrapped his arms around Maren and pulled her through the Haze, popping out again on top of a patch of weeds that had overtaken a garden of fissel plants. Jeremy lay Maren on the weeds and squinted up at the inferno growing in his castle. Thick plumes of black smoke stretched out across the sky. Lyrna appeared beside Jeremy and mewed. "How is she?" said Jeremy, pointing to Maren.

"Meow? Half plus half?"

"Be right back." In a flash, Jeremy was back in his bedroom. He started grabbing supplies and tossing them behind the air and into the Haze.

Now Jeremy was in his parents' room, and soon family heirlooms were bobbing on rays of purple. On his sixth trip, he spotted an armed guard running down the corridor. "What's going on?" shouted Jeremy.

"Cajjez Jeremy!" stammered the guard. "I've found Cajjez Jeremy!"

"What's going on!" demanded Jeremy, his fists clenched. "What's happened here?"

To Jeremy's surprise, a pack of guards rounded a corner down the hall with raised rifles. Jeremy disappeared into the Haze and slumped onto a cloud. A demon buzzed towards him and he swatted at it. "Pest."

Maren. He materialized back into the garden and landed on another patch of weeds. The weeds were an eye sore and Jeremy took a moment to trample them. "Maren?" He marched past a row of rose bushes. "Maren, you good now?" Jeremy jogged towards the courtyard with the fountain, where the sun was beaming through the smoke clouds. He expected to find her resting on a bench. "Maren?" Jeremy froze. Just beyond the first bench, past the thick hedges, someone was whispering. Jeremy ducked low and crept to the hedges.

"We'll take her to Klav, then come back," said a deep voice.

"No, someone will intercept us. They'll get the reward!"

"Well if she's telling the truth—"

"I am. It was a very precious family heirloom." It was Maren.

Jeremy crept closer and glanced around the corner. He could see two pairs of tall, laced black boots and the backs of men in uniform. Maren was just out of site.

Maren whispered and continued to reel them in. "I dropped the pouch over there. If you leave it, someone else will find the diamonds. Please, look again."

Jeremy heard an explosion to his left. More smoke in the garden. Now was his chance to get to Maren. He jumped to his feet and rounded the hedge, but wasn't the only opportunist to seize the moment of chaos.

A stampede of men charged into Maren's captors, brandishing clubs. Three bullets fired in quick succession as bodies slumped to the ground. There was screaming and then someone clubbed him on the back, knocking the wind out of him. Jeremy lay in the grass for a moment, and then sprang up. The smoke began to dissipate; Maren was gone.

"Maren!" Jeremy ran after a group of men in the distance, but didn't see Maren, and then ran after another group in the opposite direction. He caught up.

"Do you have Maren?"

The five men looked back at him in surprise. "Get him!" shouted the largest of the five, and Jeremy entered the Haze just as a bullet narrowly missed his shin.

"Lyrna! A little help? Lyrna!"

Lyrna appeared next to him. Jeremy's demons chattered in the background.

"Someone's taken Maren. My parents' Kingdom is in flames. My own guards turned on me!"

Lyrna mewed emphatically.

"I need more information." Jeremy hugged Lyrna, squeezing her tight. "Let me know if my dad or mom come through the Haze."

Lyrna bowed her head. "Alive. No sense here."

Jeremy drew in a sharp breath. "I'm going back."

Jeremy landed on Watico just outside a cottage to the west of the castle, set back into a thicket. The sky was casting strange lights and shadows, and smoke was pouring over the horizon in the distance. It was a short walk to the cottage's front door. Jeremy pounded the door and then waited. White paint was peeling off the door around the edges. If the door didn't open in three seconds, Jeremy would gladly remove it from its hinges.

The door swung open and there was a pretty young woman with midnight black hair and sad eyes. "Cajjez Jeremy!" She was dressed plainly, much like the interior of the home.

"What?" An older man appeared from behind her. "Cajjez!" They gaped at Jeremy.

"I hope you don't mind if I come in." Jeremy stepped past them. He fidgeted on their living room couch. "Where's the remote?" Jeremy groped around the couch cushions. He found the remote and clicked on the news. They all stared at the screen.

"The Leveled Ground has taken the Chikalto castle and crews are now dousing the flames and searching for bodies. Cajjez Jeremy Chikalto was sighted in the castle and is believed to be hiding in the North Tower. It has been confirmed that Vor Wantoro and Vinya Raaychila have escaped in a veiled spacecraft. Olgian Ambassador Mateo Nononia has also escaped. If anyone knows of their whereabouts, please contact your nearest militia. A reward of 50,000 Evems will be given to anyone who leads to their capture. The demons are evidently working with the royal family and are believed to be under the control of Cajjez Jeremy Chikalto. Now to Historical Scholar Broderick Savante for his controversial take on these disturbing events."

A cut-to of Broderick A. Savante, Professor of Religious Studies at Bristoli University, appeared on the screen.

"Controversial. I like that, Cindy. The demons have some affiliation with Cajjez Jeremy Chikalto. What we know is that in many incidents involving the demons, witnesses have reported that the demons said 'Jeremy Chikalto.' The family, of course, descends from the Vordin Chikalto line, and what we're looking at here is a chance for scholars such as myself to really scour some of our planet's early history to get answers. In some of our earliest scrolls dating back to 210 GAN, we read certain lines pertaining to demons, and in the Book of Gawain, we are told that Vordin Chikalto was cast down from heaven. The Book of Gawain is not considered part of the canon, but shouldn't we revisit it? If Vordin Chikalto, founder of our galaxy, was indeed a fallen angel, wouldn't that make him a demon? Suspend disbelief, Cindy, for a minute here."

"I'm sorry, so you're suggesting that there is some religious basis for what we're seeing here today in the Farmoore Galaxy? I think it's more likely we're dealing with some kind of genetically engineered soldier. Jeremy Chikalto was always a disturbed individual, and this seems like something he masterminded for his inauguration as Vor."

Broderick laughed. "Yes, that very well may be, but at Bristoli University tomorrow evening, join us for a summit—"

Jeremy shut the screen off and turned to his hosts. "So my family's been usurped?"

"Is it true about the demons?" The young woman with black hair sat down beside him on the couch. Her father tensed up.

"Cajjez Jeremy," he said, "please respect my family and leave our house. If there's anything you'd like—food, water, a change of clothes...?"

Jeremy looked down at his disheveled self. He'd been awash on Leviathan Island, inside the mouth of a monster submarine, and in battle against Mantel and his cronies. His pink button-down shirt was well past its prime, and his jeans had large chunks missing, revealing matte-black boxers. "Oh..."

"It's just that, Cajjez Jeremy, you're a danger to us here. We're already on high alert because of the fire. The guards could come here any minute."

"Take some food." The young woman jumped up off the couch and ran to the kitchen. "It's an honor to meet you. My name is Rita. Cajjez Jeremy, do you like cinkaar bars?"

Jeremy joined her in the kitchen. "I'm sorry to bring your family trouble."

Rita turned to him, her eyes glassy. "Cajjez Jeremy, please let me get you some new clothes. I'll check my brother's room." She ran from the kitchen and up the stairs, leaving Jeremy staring at the cinkaar bars. He realized he was starving, tore open the package, and devoured the crispy oatmeal snack. Next, he flung open the kitchen cabinets and poured himself a glass of water. Two glasses later, and he moved on to the refrigerator. "I'd like something hot, something I can cook up. Quick!"

The father came into the kitchen. He held up his hand to make a point, but it was shaking. "The news just

2222

reported that you were spotted in the garden outside the castle. There's a manhunt. They'll be here soon. Please, I beg you, leave."

Rita emerged with piles of clothes tucked under her arms. "He might be your size."

Jeremy eyed the frumpy pile.

"Cajjez Jeremy, once when we were little, I was invited to a royal ball in your honor. It was held in the concert hall and I remember you sang the song... what was it? 'Last night a ball of flame crackled high overhead,' something about the stars?"

Jeremy examined her brother's wardrobe and rejected each mediocre piece in a state of irritation. Maren was missing. He settled on a form-fitting navy sweater and jeans. "I should probably get a shower," he mumbled.

When Jeremy walked out of the bathroom a few minutes later, fresh as a daisy, he could hear the helicopters approaching. The father began to pray. Jeremy approached the man and his daughter and lay his hand on their shoulders. "You'll be fine. I'm leaving soon, but before I do, can you please tell me if you believe the reports." He gestured to the helicopters outside. "I thought my family was loved. My mother—how can the people of Watico turn on her? My father? People are jumping to conclusions!" Jeremy balled his fists up.

Rita looked out the window at the night sky. "If you knew about the demons, why would you cover something like that up? The Leveled Ground says that we have to band together against the royal family because a darkness follows in their steps. If you have nothing to hide, then why won't your family answer questions?" Her eyes shifted to Jeremy. "Is it true? Are there demons?"

"I suppose I could answer some questions. Yes, there are demons. My family's only just learned of them, and we're frightened and concerned, same as everyone else. But I think we'll be okay. Thank you, Rita." Jeremy left the family hiding behind their sofa, and entered the Haze.

Jeremy popped back onto Watico and strolled up to a soldier who was standing beside the brook that ran to the east of the castle.

"Excuse me," he said to the soldier. "I'd like to turn myself in to the Leveled Ground."

CHAPTER 3

LEVELED GROUND

The soldier, after doing a double take, called in an unnecessarily large group of back-up soldiers, and Jeremy was handcuffed, deposited in an armored car, and transported to the headquarters of the Leveled Ground. The headquarters were in an old Church sanctuary, west of the castle. The church stood tall, and had thick walls of limestone, with narrow doors and small windows. A harsh wind from the sea blew the thin silver trees surrounding the church back and forth. Jeremy was led through a side entrance, passing quickly through the aisles and down a trap door to a holding cell in an underground catacomb. There was a gross amount of airborne allergens hanging out in the Leveled Ground headquarters.

"A bit dramatic for an HQ."

"Shut it," snapped a guard. He jammed the butt of his rifle into Jeremy's ribs.

Jeremy's cell was small and iron bars separated him from his captors. His left hand was handcuffed to the lowest bar, forcing him to crouch. It was a blow to his well-cultivated posture. He flicked idly at the dust with his fingers.

"He won't talk!" A soldier threw his hands up and paced back and forth.

"He'll talk." A slender, tall soldier with a neatly braided beard leaned forward, just inches from Cajjez Jeremy's face. "I'll ask you one more time. How did the demons come to Watico?"

Jeremy smiled. "You'll have to torture me horribly. You'll be tried for treason, of course, and die. But go ahead. You aren't skilled enough to make me talk." Jeremy nodded at the row of torture devices set up beside his holding cell.

The bearded soldier held up an iron rod and a subordinate wheeled over a portable fire pit. The bearded soldier held the iron rod over the flame and watched it glow red. "I always savor a challenge." He pushed the rod against Jeremy's forearm and the flesh sizzled. Jeremy gritted his teeth through the pain.

"Tell me everything you know about the demons." The soldier slid the molten tip of the rod down Jeremy's arm and let it linger on Jeremy's finger. His nail began to melt and he yelped. "Okay! I'll talk!"

"I overestimated my opponent," said the soldier, disappointed with Jeremy's anti-climactic submission, and traded his rod for a hammer. He bludgeoned Jeremy's knee. Jeremy cried out.

"Okay! Let him talk!" Another soldier stepped in to cool things down.

Jeremy was reeling now, but held back his electricity. "I'll tell you everything. But first, let me see Maren. I know you've got her. Please—"

At this, the soldiers began to guffaw and slap each other on the back. "She's a bit busy with our Captain at the moment, if you know what I mean."

Jeremy tensed in his restraints.

But just then Maren rounded the corner, escorted by three soldiers.

"Maren!" shouted Jeremy.

"Jeremy!" Maren's eyes widened and she smiled with relief.

The guard nearest Jeremy sneered. "Okay, you've seen your precious, now talk."

"I want to... touch her one last time."

"How romantic! I'm getting choked up, fellas!" said the peanut gallery. The soldiers snickered.

Now Maren piped up, sensing Jeremy's plan. "If I could just hold his hand for a second? Please?"

"What a couple of disgusting saps!" One of Maren's guards spat on the ground. "Come on then, graze fingertips or whatever the hell you need to do." He led her to Jeremy's cell and everyone waited for the show. Maren's fingers slipped through the bars and made contact. Jeremy locked eyes with her, smiled, and a second later, she was floating unconscious in the Haze. The wounds on his arm shrank away and the electric throbbing of his knee vanished. He exhaled slowly and pulled Maren through again to a better spot on Watico.

They were in a dusky forest of dismow trees with an underbrush of ferns and moss. Maren drowsily came to while Jeremy stroked her cheeks.

"I'm invincible, Maren."

"No one is invincible," said Maren. "I need to sleep."

Jeremy wrapped his arms around her and they drifted off under the stars.

The next morning, Jeremy woke up early and began gathering suitable wood to build a makeshift shelter. He used a small tree with a sturdy branch as one of his anchors, and then leaned the other pieces of wood up against it, creating a nook. Then, he covered it in ferns. Maren smiled at their hut.

"I'm going to leave you again. I need you to hide in here until I get back." Jeremy held his hand up at Maren's protest. "I'm getting some supplies. We need water, food, that sort of thing. I want to minimize the Haze; it's taking a toll on your health. Lyrna will stay with you until I get back."

And Jeremy was gone. Maren waited for a time in silent repose, but then rose and began to pace. She had spent the better part of her youth in the Farmoore Galaxy studying to be an Earth Studies scholar. She knew that the University of Gilk had an extensive collection of Earthen religious texts. Maybe the answers were already in books, somewhere. How would they live out the remainder of their days? Was that something they could even control?

Jeremy appeared in front of her with two backpacks and handed her one. She opened it up and saw a new outfit folded on top. "Thanks." Maren reached past the black studded leggings and tan tunic and grabbed a bottled water.

"So I found a place," said Jeremy. "It's just through there." He pointed behind him through the thick of the forest.

Maren finished her water bottle and then squirreled it away inside her backpack. "I can't throw this onto the beautiful forest floor. Where we're going—does it have recycling?"

"It does." Jeremy laughed and then led Maren to a recently abandoned house. Though compact, it stood three stories high, and looked as pretty as the flowering trees beside it. It was painted a soft yellow and the shutters were mint green. Vespian engravings on the front door meant that it was an old house, possibly built during the reign of Vor Paul Chikalto II. Jeremy ran inside and then gestured with an air of coolness, leaning nonchalantly against a black coat rack. "Shower's upstairs, hot mess."

Maren showered, dressed, and then found herself seated across from the Cajjez in the dining room. She rolled a stress ball between her hands. "Jeremy, I think you should give the public an explanation."

Jeremy remained silent.

Maren walked to a window and pulled back the curtain. Outside, the smoke was rolling over the hills to the east. "Why do people set fires and destroy things when they want answers?" She shivered. "You need to show them your demons."

"I would cause a mass panic."

"People would be frightened, but you are powerful enough to enforce order. This chaos is far more dangerous."

Jeremy considered this, but shook his head. "It's not safe to sleep here tonight. They're probably canvassing the area." A smile spread across Jeremy's face. "How about we go somewhere with palm trees?"

Maren squinted at him. "Leviathan Island...?"

"Something like that. We'll rest, then find our parents. For sure." He held his hand out to her and she cautiously accepted.

Jeremy zipped through the Haze, pulling out at intervals for Maren's sake. His demons followed at his heels like gruesome puppies, despite Lyrna's hisses and spats. At last, Jeremy arrived at his destination. Thankfully, his demons stayed behind in the Haze.

Maren felt the warm, fresh air fill her lungs. There was no smoke here, instead the smells of rich food. Her eyes fluttered open. They were sitting on a pale beach abutting a blue ocean, with sunbathers cooking on towels nearby, high rises in the background, and the noontime sun overhead. Jeremy de-shoed his feet and worked the sand with his toes.

"I've borrowed some money just now from that nice gentleman over there." Jeremy pointed to a tall, rounded gentleman in a fashionable wide-brimmed hat. "And she helped finance our fun, too." Jeremy nodded at an older lady, clinking martinis with friends.

"You stole from them. Where are we?" asked Maren.

Jeremy laughed and made off into the crowd.

CHAPTER 4

THAT DAY AND HOUR

An hour later and Jeremy and Maren were checking in at Vista Marina, an all-inclusive resort overlooking the Mediterranean Sea.

"Your plan is Barcelona, Spain?" Maren stepped into the elevator.

"Stress clouds my judgement. We need to catch our breath." Jeremy pressed the button for the 10th floor.

Their room was a spacious suite with yellow deco walls. Lizard paintings slithered on the stone masonry, flowing along the walls to the outside balcony. Maren plopped onto a green sofa. "This is nice."

"Remember when we were six, and you told me that if you swim deep enough in the ocean, you disappear?"

"I don't remember saying something that creepy."

"'Well, that's a shame. I thought you were on to something."

Jeremy sat on the couch, lifting Maren's feet and placing them on his lap. "I actually had my castle engineer design me a deep sea diving suit because of that conversation."

Maren cooed and sunk deeper into the cushions. "I want cake."

"You deserve some cake."

"Hot chocolate."

"That too. I hear it's quite good in Spain." Jeremy jumped to his feet.

"No." Maren pushed Jeremy back onto the couch. "I'd like to go by myself."

He raised an eyebrow.

"For vacation, I'd like cake, hot chocolate, and to feel safe enough to walk the streets by myself."

Jeremy nodded. "Sounds nice."

While Maren was out, Jeremy lay on the bed, willing his demons to enter Earth's atmosphere, disappear, then reappear again. He settled on their absence, but wished the entire connection was severed. When the demons had been gone for a while, Lyrna poofed onto the bed, her head cocked to the side.

"Meow?" Lyrna leapt onto Jeremy's lap and he nuzzled her under the chin.

"I need a few drinks to loosen up."

"Drinks stink."

"Drinks do not stink, Lyrna."

Lyrna puffed slightly, then disappeared.

In a flash, Jeremy was downstairs. He walked up to a hotel employee. "Where is the bar my good man?"

The concierge smiled. "The ground level by the pool." His Spanish accent was thick, but his English was impeccable.

"Why thank you." Jeremy followed the signs for the pool. He strolled down a winding staircase that led outside and breathed in the fresh salt air. Jeremy slid past the large in-ground pool and made his way to the tiki bar. He drummed on the counter and admired the gin and tonic the bartender was making. She juiced an orange slice over the dry liquor.

"Yes, señor?" She slid the drink to another patron and smiled at Jeremy.

Jeremy disappeared behind the air and reappeared behind the bar. He snatched the top-shelf champagne, scotch, bourbon, and something sweet-looking in a bejeweled flask. The bartender gasped, and he was gone.

Back in the hotel room, Jeremy was lounging on the couch, sipping champagne. Then the door opened and an amused Maren came in.

"Maren, look at what I've got." Jeremy hopped off the couch and pulled a purple sheet dramatically off his stash of goods. The champagne bottle teetered and Jeremy dove towards it. "Oops!" He steadied it and faced Maren.

"Very nice," she said. Maren placed her cake next to the bottles, along with grapes, salsa, chips, guacamole and cheese.

Together they feasted, indulged, and imbibed. After a few toasts, they reclined in their chairs on the balcony and watched the sun set.

"We should just live here. I'll bring our families, we'll live in obscurity; it'll be beautiful.

"When we find them we will," replied Maren, stretching her arms overhead.

Jeremy took another sip. "I was sitting with Lyrna earlier and it made me think.... I could find a suitable ball of fluff with supernatural dimension-crossing powers just for you. They come in handy in times of Apocalypse."

Maren swiped Jeremy's glass from his hand and dumped the bubbly liquid down her throat. "What spirit animal would suit me?"

"A fox."

Maren smiled.

"You're cunning and your feet are so small." Jeremy picked up one of Maren's feet and kissed it. "I've always loved your feet."

"Thank you. I've always enjoyed your..." Maren slinked over to Jeremy's seat and sat on his lap. "Your voice."

"Well I am an intergalactic singer—"

"Yes, but I mean the way you talk. There's a soothing quality to it. And when you speak low, there's a slight gravely edge. When I'm close," she lifted his shirt up and pressed her cheek against his chest, "I can feel the vibrations."

"Tipsy Maren is very bold."

She leaned forward and began to kiss his chest, working her way down. She stopped just above the top button of his jeans.

Jeremy sighed and slid his fingers through Maren's

hair. He pulled her face to his, cradling her chin delicately in his fingertips, and kissed her.

The next morning, Maren woke up first. Her eyes would open, but she would drift back into the feather mattress. She dreamt of milk in a bucket, which was divided into quadrants, one red, one blue, one yellow, and one green. The surface of the milk thickened, as all the cream rose to the top. Then she saw that the sky was falling, and the cream evaporated. In dreams, the Haze mixed with the mind and told riddles.

At last, Maren sat upright and rubbed her eyes. She looked beside her at Jeremy—her Jeremy. She leaned forward and brushed his cheek. Then someone screamed outside and she jumped. Jeremy jolted up in bed.

Maren crept to the window. An old woman was outside in the alley between the white buildings, sobbing, her face in her hands. A frowning man walked over to her and put his arm around her shoulder, and they disappeared together inside a high-rise hotel across the street. Maren let out a breath of air she'd been holding and looked to Jeremy.

"I hope everything is all right," he offered in a hushed voice. He slid out of bed and wrapped his arms around Maren. "We're still on vacation."

Two hours later, they decided on snorkeling. The hotel was strangely empty, and there was no concierge at the desk downstairs. They left the hotel and walked down the street towards the beach, a block away. Before hitting the sand, they stopped at a surf shop to rent some gear. The shop was small and colorful, with baskets full of sea shells and pretty stones by the door, and jewelry displayed in a large wooden chest in the center of the room. Surf boards, flippers, snorkels, masks, and floats lined the walls, and a TV was positioned above the counter. The shopkeeper wouldn't look them in the eye, and absently handed them flippers, masks, and snorkels. As Jeremy and Maren left the shop, they heard a muffled cry. Maren gave Jeremy a worried smile.

The beach was empty, and the sun was making them pleasantly hot. Jeremy pulled out the flippers, masks, and snorkels from his backpack while Maren stripped to her bathing suit. Jeremy pretended not to watch. They donned their gear and flip-flopped like a couple of penguins into the halcyon ocean.

The water was brisk, blue and calm, but they were kicking up too much sand and scaring away the fish.

"Let's go over there." Maren flippered forward and swam into the vastness. Jeremy followed her. They went farther out, until their flippers couldn't reach the ocean floor. The ocean around them was indigo.

"Not scared?" asked Jeremy.

"Nope." Maren ducked below the water.

Jeremy turned and twisted to try to see her figure under the depths. All he could see was the blue water, the white caps rolling along the surface. He dove down into the depths for a time and counted the seconds...one...two...three...four...five. But he was never one for patience. He resurfaced and took his mask off. "Maren," he called out.

A slosh of water gurgled up beside him. He watched it expectantly. His pulse quickened. "Maren!" he yelled. She appeared behind him.

"It's okay," she said, placing her hands on his shoulders. "Are you okay?"

"Yeah. What were you doing, looking for treasures?"

Maren tilted her head to the side. "I didn't see much. Even real deep where the pressure hurts my ears—I don't know—it feels empty." She squinted up at the sun and pushed her hair back off her face. "I'm ready to head in."

"Me too."

When they got back to the street beyond the beach, people were gathered together in small clusters, talking in low voices. A man on a bike whizzed by Maren and Jeremy, brushing Maren's shoulder as he passed. He jumped off the bike and ran along side it and into a group of people. The circle of people opened up to receive him and soon they were all embracing.

"I guess we should just drop these off then," said Jeremy, gesturing to the snorkeling gear and trying his best not to stare at the crowd.

"Yeah." Maren ducked into the surf shop and led the way to the counter. Everyone in the store was watching a TV positioned in the corner of the store just above the register.

The news was playing in Spanish, one of the Earth languages Maren neglected to learn. The anchor seemed nervous, and there were pictures of numerous people stacking up to his left in a news graphic.

"Here," Maren lifted the snorkeling gear onto the counter. The man behind the register didn't even look her way. She glanced back at Jeremy.

"We already paid earlier," he said softly, "so we can just... go." He glanced at the TV screen. A woman was describing a first-hand experience. Tears were streaming down her face, and she kept throwing her arms up, yelling "Tragedia!"

Maren walked back outside and Jeremy followed.

"It was a missing person's report, or a series of them I guess," said Jeremy when they were on the sidewalk that led back to their hotel.

Maren shifted uncomfortably. "Yeah. It seems to be a big story. Hey, so I'd like to buy some new shoes."

"Of course." Jeremy and Maren were walking through the shopping district now, just behind the hotels. Colorful, eclectic stores lined the street. They walked into a shoe store.

Jeremy patted her on the back. "Something practical, in case we have to flee," he said with a fake laugh. People were standing in a back room, watching news on the TV.

"Got it. I hate the way sneakers look on me, though."

Jeremy lifted up a pair of zebra-striped high-tops. "These look like you."

Maren smiled but then noticed that an old man in the back was staring at her. She was horrified to realize that more people were staring. "I don't actually need shoes."

"You do. And you will get shoes."

Maren backed towards the store exit.

Jeremy sighed and grabbed a pair of gray high tops. A single, purple paw print was sewn onto the side of each shoe. "These are you. Size, Maren?"

"I don't need it."

"Size," he repeated louder, more stern. When she didn't respond, he walked over to her, yanked her shoe off and located the size. She hobbled uncomfortably on one foot. Jeremy walked irritably to the counter and paid for the shoes. The clerk was distracted. As he turned to walk out of the store, a man grabbed his wrist.

"Hey idioto!" shouted the man, black hair curling out from under his bandana. "You good? Comprende?" he called back to Maren.

"Yes, I'm good." Maren's voice was a little more singsongy than she'd meant.

Jeremy squinted viciously at the man and jerked his arm back. "You've no idea what we've been through."

"Has visto las noticias? News?" The man jabbed a finger to the TV. The customers in the store seemed to swell in size and stature.

"Yes, I get it, something bad happened," shouted Jeremy. "I'm sorry you feel the need to take it out on me." He backed out of the store.

"Adios," said the shopkeeper. "Go home to families! Adios!" he repeated. He waved everyone out of his store. "La tienda esta cerrada!"

Maren ushered Jeremy towards her. "Gracias." She grabbed Jeremy's hand. "Let's just go." She led Jeremy quickly down an alley.

"Smart, Maren," said Jeremy. "People are acting all weird and you want to go down a shady alley."

"Do you hear yourself, Jeremy?" Maren crossed her arms and leaned against the brick wall of the store. "They are no threat to you."

"But—"

"Something's going on and we have to find out what. Come." Maren took his hand and led Jeremy through to the other side of the alley. The clouds were dispersing, and the sun shone brightly in the sky. The street was swarming with talking people now, and the fear was audible.

Then there was a great rumble, and the ground began to shake violently, knocking the crowd to the ground. Glass was shattering all over the place, and people were screaming. A building down the street crashed down. And then it was still.

Jeremy and Maren hopped to their feet, and people around them began to moan. There was blood and glass shards on the ground. A siren pierced the air, blaring from a speaker in the shopping district, and Jeremy and Maren covered their ears. Then another building collapsed down the street, and someone fired a gun. The shot seemed to freeze everyone for a time, and then the stampede began. Men and women screamed and fled in every direction. Jeremy and Maren ducked into a nearby art gallery and rushed into the back. "I just need a second to think!" began Jeremy. An old man with dark skin and white whiskers hobbled over to them from behind huge canvasses. He massaged the beads of his rosary and spoke to them in a thick accent. "But of that day and hour no one knows, no, not even the angels of heaven, but My Father only." He had sad, bloodshot eyes. "All the good ones are gone now. Gone!"

CHAPTER 5

THE VIOLENCE OF EACH WAVE

Maren gasped. "The missing people on the news."

"The Rapture?" asked Jeremy.

The old man nodded and limped into a side room behind a curtain. The lights in the store flickered and then went out.

Jeremy looked down at the blue aura emanating from his hands.

An aftershock jolted the floor, and the screams outside peaked. Jeremy and Maren walked through the artwork over to the cracked windows, and a few men ran past them into the store, grabbing as many canvasses as they could and running out.

"Revelations talks about a leader who will be revealed soon after the Rapture."

"Am I...?"

"The Antichrist." Maren blurted the words out. "No! I mean, the coming world leader is sometimes *referred* to as the Antichrist. Not you!"

Jeremy stood up. "You said it yourself, Maren." He looked outside. "Do you hear that?"

Through the blare of the siren, a voice spoke in a clear tone. "Alerta de Tsunami. Por favor, busque refugio sobre el nivel del mar. Tsunami Warning. Please seek shelter above sea level." The message continued to loop.

"Should I show my demons?" He turned to her. "A reign of terror is still better than chaos. That's what you said, right?"

"Jeremy!" Maren waved him back to her. "This is madness. Take us to the hotel, now!"

The two disappeared into the Haze. A minute later, they were in the hotel room. They heard gunfire, and Maren made sure the door was bolted. The sirens continued to blare and Jeremy ran to the balcony to look at the sea. He shielded his brow with his hand and squinted at the horizon. "I don't see the tsunami."

"Do you believe it?" Maren asked as she walked to the balcony. "That all the true believers were transported to Heaven?" She paused. "The Greeks believed that souls are ferried to the land of the dead. In accounts of astral projection, subjects are connected to their bodies by a chord. Each story is like a lens that brings things into focus, and when they are stacked vertically, the clarity multiplies."

Maren left the balcony, and Jeremy pondered the expanse of the ocean and the violence of each wave.

CHAPTER 6

APEX

The next morning, Jeremy poured himself and Maren a glass of orange juice. At least the electricity and their mini-fridge were still working. Jeremy was keeping it well-stocked with choice looting around the world. It was a strange night, but the hotel seemed relatively safe. Maren took a bite of her egg croissant and stared out the window. The hotel was a ghost town, and the beach was empty.

Jeremy turned on the TV, and it began to stream the latest news in English, from the UK.

"Late Friday night, billions are believed to have disappeared or else remain unaccounted for. It seems every family has parted with some relative, and in certain areas, entire families have disappeared. The World Health Network has cautioned that this might be a plague, with the virus causing a fast-acting breakdown of the human body in a matter of minutes. NATO believes a chemical agent is to blame. Some religious leaders believe this to be the Rapture. NATO agents are on the ground conducting tests for trace chemical agents in the air and in water supplies. For the time being, everyone is advised to stay indoors until more information is available."

Jeremy clicked the TV off and sighed. "So where to next, boss?" He stood up and turned the radio on. Techno beats bumped from the speakers and Jeremy started doing jumping jacks.

Maren laughed. "Jumping jacks and demons? You are quite the specimen."

"You should do some too, they clear your head." Jeremy jumping jacked over to Maren and lifted her up to her feet. She joined him in a few half-hearted jumping jacks and then stopped.

"It's the end of the world and you still need booze to let loose? Tomorrow morning, we'll drink mimosas." Jeremy started doing squat jumps.

Maren looked at her toes. She wished to paint them. But even more so than that, she wished to paint her whole body—in the nude. "Honestly, Jeremy," she slid out of her pants, "I don't have the same humors as you. I'm calm. To me freedom feels like this." She pulled her shirt off over her head. "In my last hours, I'd like to be naked."

Jeremy was smiling ear to ear. "And in the daylight! I could die like this, too."

Maren walked over to the sofa and lay on it.

"So...?" Jeremy sat at attention on the edge of the cushion.

Maren smiled at him. "I just want to sit and enjoy

being naked—this is not for you, though you've been trained to think that way." She rolled her eyes. "It's hot outside, and I'd love to just lay here for a moment. Go finish your uninhibited jumping jacks."

Jeremy had to slap himself on the cheeks a few times to take his eyes off of Maren and leave her be. He understood her desire and wanted to respect her. But it wasn't easy considering the circumstances.

The morning sun had reached its apex. Maren put her clothes back on while Jeremy doodled geese on the walls of the hotel with a pen he'd found in the nightstand drawer beside the bed.

Maren interrupted the artistic genius. "So I'm thinking our parents might be on my home planet, Olg."

Jeremy leaned back against the wall. "Quite possible, assuming there's still chaos on Watico."

"There is. Do you think the Rapture affected the Farmoore Galaxy?"

Jeremy considered this. "I'm not sure. We're of Judas's stock, so to speak."

"Vordin Chikalto repented. That has to count for something."

"Let's go find out."

Maren nodded and they disappeared into the Haze.

Jeremy raced her through, crossing dimensions at top speed. In his peripheral vision, he saw that his demons were rallying again. The spirit animals kept their distance.

Below him, a boar was running circles in a purple-gray cloud, seemingly out of boredom. No souls were visible.

Jeremy pulled out. They were on a distant planet in the Farmoore Galaxy, but still had another stop before reaching the planet Olg. The sky was a burnt orange and insects buzzed in the tall grass. Maren took a breath and Jeremy watched her intently. He sat in silence, trying to decipher the change that was taking place in the Haze. While Maren stabilized, Jeremy took a peek behind the veil.

He was on a dark purple vapor, drifting downwards. A hyena's laugh echoed all around him. "Lyrna!" he called. A few spirit animals swam towards him, sniffing the air, until a demon floated to him and stretched itself thin, as waify as a sheet of paper. Jeremy got lost in the dark, wide 'O' of its mouth. He pulled away and settled on a lighter cloud of pink. "It feels empty in here." Jeremy shooed away a raccoon who was eyeing up his chest. "What?" The critter started to claw at him. "I don't have a chord," he said.

The raccoon looked puzzled and floated away. A lot of spirit animals had stopped their meandering to watch the exchange. *What was missing?* No souls were passing through the Haze. The animals spirits were without charge.

Then Lyrna swiped at Jeremy's back. "Mew."

He turned to face her. "Why are so many spirit animals idle?"

"Dead turned away."

"Oh? So... are they ghosts?"

Lyrna shrugged.

Jeremy swished away a dark purple cloud that had begun to form in front of his face. "I have to take Maren through to Olg." Lyrna nodded and Jeremy returned to Maren's side. He embraced her from behind and pulled her back through.

Minutes later, they were on the planet Olg, just outside Maren's family castle. Wet green fields glistened in the mid-morning sun. The castle was set on a high, rolling hill, and towns rose up in small clusters further out, closer to the sea.

Jeremy palmed his forehead. "Probably should be a bit more discreet." A guard standing watch at the metal gate flinched at their sudden appearance, but otherwise remained in place.

Jeremy smiled at the guard, waved, and then fanned Maren's face. She opened her eyes and he shook her slightly. "Hey," he called out to the guard. "I'm Cajjez Jeremy Chikalto. I've brought Maren home safely. Let us through."

The guard, who was wearing white body armor and a helmet, his hand firmly planted on his sword, only wavered a little.

Jeremy was about to raise his voice when Maren pushed her way out of Jeremy's arms and approached the guard. "Ren Golsen? Where is my father? Let us in."

The guard leaned forward slightly. "You're being monitored by video. Leave, now."

Maren shook her head. "But—"

"So then we've already been spotted," said Jeremy. He steadied Maren, placing a hand on her shoulder. She hadn't recovered fully from Haze travel.

"You haven't. The guards would be here by now if you had," said the guard.

Maren scanned the few trees on the property. "So you'll be punished when they see the video."

"Yes."

Maren turned to Jeremy. "He's got to come with us."

"Miss Nononia, I cannot leave my post."

"He cannot leave his post," repeated Jeremy. "Let's just leave."

"Whose command are you currently following?" asked Maren.

"Today, His Highness Lawrence Chandler; yesterday, Captain Vallary of the Leveled Ground, Chapter III," he said with contempt.

Maren grabbed Ren's wrist and yanked him forward. "You're coming with us."

"My family..."

Maren frowned. "Where is your family?"

"35 Wantin Park, Estelle Gardens, Pathway #7."

"About twenty miles north," said Maren. "North is that way," she added impatiently, pointing.

Jeremy grabbed Maren and the guard and pulled them through to the Haze, pushing a crowd of spirit animals out of his way. A stubborn mule stood its ground and opened its mouth to chomp at the guard's leg, baring grisly red gums. Jeremy yanked Ren away from the teeth. "Hey! They aren't dead. Just passing through!" A demon hissed nearby and the mule trotted away.

Jeremy popped out of the Haze and sat on the grass while Maren and Ren came to.

They were at the edge of a meadow beside a brook. Jeremy grabbed a slimy stone and skipped it across the water with impeccable technique.

Ren was the first to speak. "How are we here?"

"Strange times," said Jeremy, jumping to his feet. "I just saved you from about thirty mauling weasels."

"Just down here, Ren?" Maren pointed to a lane just past the meadow, which curled into a mass of small saplings.

"Yes," he said.

The young man lifted off his helmet to reveal shoulder-length black hair. His face was porcelain white and his eyes were wide-set and brown. Jeremy felt a dull weight settle on his chest: could Ren be more handsome than himself? Jeremy could feel his own face tense up, and he almost unleashed a verbal assault on the man's appearance or posture or proposed livelihood, but held his tongue. *Still the best.*

"How did I get here, Miss Nononia?" asked Ren. He stepped onto the dirt pathway that wound through the trees, and the three started walking.

"We have a secret way of teleporting, more or less. You're safe with us. And call me Maren."

To Jeremy's surprise, Ren did not press her for more.

Maren held Jeremy's hand and smiled. "I've known Ren for a long, long time and both he and his family are very loyal to the Nononias. Ren," she continued, "do you know if my father and Jeremy's parents are hiding on the planet Olg?"

"Not that I know of, Maren. Your family's guards remain loyal, as do most of the staff at the Nononia castle, but we've been infiltrated—first by the Leveled Ground, and then by a local militia. The militia has ties with the Labor Party, which is loyal, but there's some talk of a few defectors ranking higher up who might turn you over to the Leveled Ground if the price is right."

"Thank you, Ren. Your family will receive full amnesty from any charges of insubordination, once this mess is straightened out."

Ren hesitated and ducked below a low tree branch. "Thank you, Miss—er, Maren." The idea of anything being straightened out seemed implausible lately.

Maren leaned in toward Ren. "Have people... disappeared here lately? Like, en masse?"

Ren shook his head.

"I see." Maren sighed.

Jeremy whistled a sad tune.

The wind picked up and flower petals twirled to life, encircling the party.

They walked for ten minutes down the quiet lane to the Golsen residence. The large blue house was dome-shaped and Jeremy, Maren, and Ren walked around it to the back, where they met an expansive parking lot packed with hover-cars.

"That's quite the collection," said Jeremy.

"Yes, my dad is passionate." Ren cleared his throat and then headed to the front door. Ren's mother, a heavy-set woman with short black hair, flung the front door open and bounded towards them with open arms. She gave Maren a bear hug.

"Have your families come to Olg? Has your father reclaimed the castle?" asked Ren's mother.

"No," said Maren, watching the woman's face fall.

"Is everything all right? Do you bring news?"

"We've been granted amnesty," said Ren.

The woman's brows knitted together, and her eyes grew wide. "Are we in trouble?"

Ren fidgeted. "I'm afraid Miss Nononia and Cajjez Jeremy came to the castle when I was standing guard."

"I see." Ren's mother frowned. "Well don't just stand there, come in! I'll go get your father."

Ren's mother, Amelia, a hearty woman with rosy cheeks, set down the plates and silverware, while his father, Takumi, took a seat beside Jeremy.

"Go to the cellar and get our guests some wine. We have a lot to talk about," said Takumi. Takumi's hair was impeccably parted down the middle, his grays showcased like trophies.

Ren nodded and went downstairs.

When the table was set and the wine was poured, Jeremy forgot his princely table etiquette and gobbled up the roasted potatoes, febcrum, and red peppers. "Sorry," he said after he'd cleared his plate.

"Don't be ridiculous, I'm happy to put some meat on those bones, Cajjez," said Amelia, tsk-tsking at Jeremy's wiry build. She smiled, took his plate, and heaped another helping of stew onto the porcelain.

"The demon sightings," began Ren, but he didn't know where to go from there.

"It's okay, we need to clear the air," said Maren. "It's true. There are demons."

"And do they call to Cajjez Jeremy?" Takumi sipped his wine and eased the glass down.

"They did," said Jeremy, "but they're gone now. You don't have to fret yourself anymore."

Maren bit her lip and turned to Jeremy.

"Contained," said Jeremy, "gone... in a manner of speaking," he added, leaning back in his chair.

Ren stood up and poured himself a glass of water. He offered the pitcher to Maren and she politely declined. "It was wrong of the Leveled Ground to capitalize on this chaos. I've seen loyal men and women turn on Ambassador Mateo. On Mateo!"

"Politics," Jeremy stood up and stretched, "are a headache. A few tribesmen, bickering over who the biggest hut belongs to, while lions gather outside the village."

Amelia's brows furrowed and she placed a protective hand on her son's shoulders.

"I'm afraid he's right," said Maren. "Now's the time to look after your loved ones. Beware of power, because in dark times, the weak rule."

The rest of the evening passed by in talk of old times, and soon Jeremy and Maren were set up in the guest room. It was a small room with two quaint paintings of green fields on light yellow walls. A ceiling fan whirred overhead. While in bed, Jeremy placed his arm around Maren and encapsulated them both in a blue force field. Maren giggled. "What are you doing?"

"Can you feel the buzz?" Jeremy nuzzled his head into her neck.

"That tickles," she said. "I'm tired, turn out your light." She smiled.

"I'll sleep soon. I just need to feel safe for a moment. Let me have this buzz."

Maren grunted and turned away from him, fading fast into sleep. Jeremy thought for some time on Maren's words at dinner. Ten minutes later, he let his force field fizzle out and fell asleep.

CHAPTER 7

THE IN-CROWD

At 2:30 a.m. in the Civic Center district of San Francisco, down in the depths of the BART station, a grizzled man stumbled and swayed his way to a bench. He was singing a song, chuckling through the verses and pulling on his stringy hair. His soiled sweatshirt read, "He is coming, pray for forgiveness."

"La, la, la, they don't want you to know about the vampires, they want to make you pay taxes, but I know the spaceship is coming, it's in the Constitution...." He closed his eyes and lay on the bench, enjoying his echoes in the empty station. The lights flickered, and then there was a blinding flash. He sat up, and the whole subway station was suddenly like a bomb threat at rush hour, people packed tight and panicking.

"I knew it."

CHAPTER 8

LEAVING

"Should I open the fridge and close it obnoxiously?" Jeremy tapped the fridge door.

"They'll be up soon. I can't imagine they slept well, knowing they're about to leave their lives behind."

"I did," said Jeremy. He took a moment to rearrange some of the fridge magnets.

"We're just... a little more seasoned." Maren looked at the clock on the wall. A floor board creaked.

Thirty minutes later, and still the hosts had not risen. Maren poised herself outside Ren's door.

"Do it," goaded Jeremy.

Maren knocked.

No answer.

"Ren? We should probably get going."

Still no answer.

Jeremy grabbed the door handle and pushed the door open. "Hey, Ren my boy."

The young guard was not in his room.

"They've left us!" Maren raced down the hallway and rapped on Ren's parents' door. "Hello? We should probably be heading out."

No answer.

Jeremy smiled. "It's perfectly understandable. We have no power, we're wanted by, well, *everybody*, and you offer them amnesty."

"We *do* have power!"

"They don't know that. The way they see it, they're sitting ducks with us."

"You don't know the Golsen family! They are *loyal*."

Jeremy tapped Maren on the nose. "You're cute when you're naive."

Jeremy grabbed a handful of car keys off a shelf despite Maren's protesting, and made his way out back to the hovercar collection. He tried the keys until he found one that matched the solar-powered VEX Hovercar Special Edition with booster mods, the "sweet one," as Jeremy put it. Jeremy hopped gleefully into the driver's seat and Maren reluctantly joined him.

Jeremy floored the pedal and the VEX flew down the long parking lot, the air brakes whining at the sharp turn onto the road. "Love the countryside," said Jeremy, racing down the road winding through the woods.

Maren released her breath. "Easy."

There was a bend in the road and Jeremy hugged its edge, accelerating.

"Knock it off!"

Jeremy just winked.

"You like torturing me for some reason," said Maren. "Just drive regular so we don't get pulled over."

"Low profile, yeah, yeah." He slowed the car and then turned the radio on—static. "What, no music?"

Maren surfed through the frequencies: Static. Static. Some high-pitched white noise. She turned it off.

Then they smelled the smoke.

Maren covered her sleeve over her face as the car took a left turn onto a main stretch of highway that bisected a field.

Up ahead, a car had flipped onto its side. Jeremy passed it slowly, but didn't see any bodies.

Jeremy pointed to the intersection. "There's another one. And another."

"Are they okay?" Maren gripped the dashboard.

Jeremy made a u-turn and drove in the opposite direction. The car approached a traffic light where five cars were lined up, hovering. "Let's just have a look." Jeremy stopped the car ten feet back from the nearest one. He hopped out and made his way towards another solar-powered VEX Hover-car Special Edition, without booster mods. Static blasted from the car's radio and the frequency hurt his ears. He searched the interior but the car was empty.

"What is it?" Maren called out.

"Nothing." Jeremy walked up to the next car. It was a silver, large enough to accommodate a family of six. He looked inside the back window. There were two empty car seats. The front seats were empty too.

Jeremy ducked back into the car with Maren and stared blankly ahead. "Everyone's gone. How about we just check back on Watico." The wind picked up and they could see storm clouds rolling closer in the distance.

Maren nodded.

Jeremy leaned across his seat and placed a hand on Maren's shoulder. He brought her through the Haze and into the Chikaltos' royal garden, which was showing signs of neglect. All around, the green plants wilted; the delicate petals of the benitia flowers curled up, their tips a dreadful burnt-orange. There was no movement, no noise beyond the wind. Jeremy lifted his arms up and felt the strange energy of the place. "Do you feel the absence of life?"

"I... suppose so." Maren rubbed her arms. "I feel cold," she said softly.

"Let's have a look inside." Jeremy motioned to his castle. "I don't think there's anyone here."

Maren nodded and braced herself.

They made their way slowly down a snaking cobblestone path towards the south side of the castle. At the side entrance, the door was ajar. Nobody was manning their posts. "Hello?" called Jeremy, peeking in the door. "Your Cajjez has returned." His inflection was sing-songy, and when it echoed back to him he felt sick. "They're not here."

Jeremy dashed forward through the doors and up a long, steep staircase, the bannisters charred from the recent fire. "Come on!" he yelled back to Maren. He disappeared from view.

"Jeremy?" Maren turned a corner. She'd entered the west wing. She stepped over the ashes of what was once an antique hand-dyed rug. "Where are you? I don't know my way around!"

Maren stopped in front of his bedroom door, charred black. She heard a rustling noise. "Are you in there?" She pressed her ear against the door. The noise was getting louder. "Jeremy!" There was a thud. Now something was beating on the exterior of the castle. Maren pressed her back to the wall, her heart fluttering in her chest. Jeremy flung the door open. He'd been crying and was covered in a green velvet cape, several cloaks, and jewelry, fortuitously preserved but reeking of smoke.

"What are you doing!" Maren pulled Jeremy forward.

"There's something outside," said Jeremy. The noise had sobered him, but he still looked insane. The wind picked up to a feverish pitch. The curtains ripped off, and debris from the burnt castle whipped around outside. Rare glass objects crashed off Jeremy's shelves.

"Close the window!" shouted Maren.

"Aren't you supposed to leave the window open?"

"I don't remember!"

A strong gust blew through and shattered glass everywhere. A lamp flung across the room and crashed against the wall inches from Maren's head. Trees were uprooted from outside and the entire castle was shaking now, trembling and rumbling. It tipped left, then right.

The sky lit up and a bright orange light filled the room. Suddenly the air felt warm, then hot. Jeremy tried to close his bedroom door, as though that might save them. He battled it with massive force, and the blue energy crackled off his body. The murals on the wall behind him warped in the heat.

"Jeremy! We have to leave now!" Maren was wedged behind a curio.

Jeremy dashed to her. The light was blinding now. He grabbed her arm and pulled her through to the Haze. Jeremy raced with her through the purple swirls of light, ignoring the curious paws that stretched out to his exotic green cape. In a panic, he could feel in the Haze that all the planets in the Farmoore Galaxy were exploding or imploding or else disappearing completely from his awareness. There'd be nowhere to pull Maren out for oxygen: he needed Earth's atmosphere.

Luckily for Maren, Jeremy's desperation electrified his speed. He blasted forward like a rocket, and in a few moments Jeremy found himself back in New York City.

CHAPTER 9

GLOBE OF DUST AND SMOKE

Jeremy and Maren were just outside Tina's house on Fifth Avenue in New York. It looked to be about five in the afternoon, and the sky was a globe of dust and smoke. Hundreds of people were shouting all around them, demanding to be let inside Tina's home. A ring of armed, military-garbed men were pushing people back, beckoning others forward. An older woman was led by the arm through a line of soldiers and the door to Tina's brown stone apartment was opened for her. There was a rumbling in the distance.

"Move back!" shouted a man through a megaphone. The crowd scattered and a black tank the size of a house emerged from around the block, the sidewalk cracking beneath its treads, its huge cannon dragging down cancer-walk banners that were strung overhead. Jeremy flung a half-conscious Maren over his shoulder and ran over to a man in uniform. "I have to see Tina! Let me through."

Common courtesy seemed antiquated given the state of things, so Jeremy disappeared before hearing what the man had to say and then reappeared in Tina's kitchen. It would have been an open space, with lustrous white beams partitioning the kitchen off from the rest of the house, except for all the people crowded around the perimeter. Tina's parents were standing in front of the television arguing. Tina was in the living room hugging a crying friend. Her brown, curly hair was slicked back in an elegant french braid, and she had glitter on her chest, which rubbed off on everyone she touched.

Jeremy steadied Maren and then led her over to Tina. He tapped her on the shoulder and she turned around, eyes wide and brows knitted.

"Oh. My. God!" She hugged Maren and then Jeremy, plumes of glitter cascading all around the reunion like confetti. "So happy you made it!" She groped and embraced Maren, then Jeremy, then Maren again. "Don't worry, we'll get going soon. My daddy will take care of us." Just then Frisky walked through the door and set down a large hiking backpack beside the staircase. She pushed her brown hair behind her ears and adjusted her glasses.

"You're here!" Tina launched into another elaborate greeting.

Jeremy and Maren waited while the commotion around them escalated. Family members were still arriving and soon they were all packed like sardines.

"Close it up, we're done here!" shouted a booming voice—it was Tina's father, a man with a strict military cut and buff forearms, who was waving at a line of soldiers.

Tina pushed through to her father and clung to him. "You're leaving now?"

"Yes, pumpkin. I'll see you when the dust settles." He kissed her on the forehead.

"Move out!" A circle of soldiers formed around Tina's father, and then they burst through the front door and ran to one of the big tanks parked out front.

Tina was nibbling at her fingernails. The door closed, and they were gone. She ran back to Jeremy and Maren. "We'll see him later." She nodded to herself. "Follow me. Nice outfit, Jeremy."

Jeremy, Maren, and Frisky followed Tina through the endless ebb and flow of people, up the stairs, and into Tina's bedroom. The room was spacious and shaped like an "L." Tina's king-sized bed was draped in a purple leopard print comforter. The hardwood floor looked freshly polished. The room wrapped around to a private bathroom enclave with a small window. Tina let out a big sigh. "So, hi! Welcome."

Maren took a seat on the floor and let her fingers play with the plush, neon pink rug beneath her. "What's going on?"

Jeremy sat down beside her and placed a reassuring hand on her leg, but Frisky, sitting across from them, shot him a prudish look.

"A lot," said Frisky, crossing her arms.

Maren beamed at her mousy friend. "Frisky, you're a survivor!"

"We're safe because of money. Most of the people I know aren't so lucky." Frisky's eyes welled up, and she wiped them on the sleeve of her eggshell cardigan. "But yes, thank God. I don't mean to be a downer."

"Where were you when it happened? Did anyone pop into your room?" Tina leaned forward, ready for a story.

Frisky was silent but shook her head.

"I'm sorry, what?" said Jeremy.

"Well," Tina jumped up on her bed for effect. "There I was, enjoying dinner with my beloved family, when BAM! Or no, wait, I went to the bathroom. I was holding my pee in because my mom ordered this sweet lemon tart cake from this bakery that was still open after everyone disappeared—talk about customer loyalty, am-I-right?" She jumped up and down some more.

"Go on," said Maren.

"So I was in the bathroom—mid-pee, when BAM!" Tina made a gun with her hand and shot three times. "Three of them, speaking all gobbly-gook!"

Jeremy and Maren waited patiently.

"Your turn," said Tina, taking a seat on her bed.

"We have no idea what you're talking about," said Maren.

"We weren't here," said Jeremy, "until just now. We were in the Farmoore Galaxy, on my home planet." Which was no more. He swallowed hard.

"A couple of hours ago, suddenly, like millions of people appeared out of nowhere!" Tina was shouting, excited to be the first to deliver the news. "Millions! Maybe billions. Did you see how crowded it is out there?"

"People?" asked Jeremy. "So the Rapture happened, and then... everyone came back?"

"No, these people are different. Over here," Frisky stood up and walked to Tina's window. "Look outside."

Jeremy and Maren followed her to the small window. Fifth Avenue was a sea of people clawing at one another, like a World Series win celebrated by zombies.

"Oh dear," whispered Maren.

Tina stepped behind them and put her arms around Jeremy and Maren. "But I told my dad everything about Leviathan Island, about the Maze, and the demons. He didn't believe me at first, of course, but after the Rapture happened, he decided to fortify our beach house in the Hamptons just in case. I mean, it's only been a couple of days, but we're rockin' and rollin'!"

"Money, so much money!" Frisky pretended to maul her eyes out.

"Money is going to save your ass," said Tina. "My dad used to be in the military too, so he was able to tap into that real quick, once the government, well, you know."

"They don't know," Frisky deadpanned.

Tina slapped her cheek. "Right, so the President was assassinated earlier today, the Vice President too. Politicians everywhere are dropping like flies. People are revolting, all kinds of religious groups are taking over."

"There are just too many people now," said Frisky.

Maren drew back from the window. "This is sad."

"Want to hear want happened to my home planet?" asked Jeremy.

CHAPTER 10

LURCH FORWARD

That night, Jeremy, Maren, Frisky, and Tina all slept in Tina's room. There was a lot of shouting outdoors and a lot of crying indoors. Tina's mother, Anna—a curvy woman with cat-shaped glasses and large, curly hair, flicked the light switch on just as the first ray of dull sunshine filtered in through the curtains.

"Get up, Tina. Everyone, we're putting you on the next tank. Hope you slept well."

Tina popped up out of bed immediately and shouted about peeing, while Jeremy, Maren, and Frisky groggily came to.

Frisky sat up on her elbows and rubbed her eyes. "Did anyone else smell cotton candy all night?"

Jeremy lifted up a perfume dispenser that was sitting on Tina's nightstand. "Yes."

Downstairs, everyone was handed a simple breakfast —a packaged muffin and bottled water. Then there was a great roar, and soldiers burst into the room, shouting and waving everyone forward. Jeremy and Maren got swept into the herd, which made its way outside. The street was momentarily clear in front of the apartment steps, and the lucky few ran up a ramp and into the massive tank. The doors were sealed and the vehicle lurched forward. Other smaller tanks followed.

The inside of the main tank was surprisingly roomy and well-lit. The recently reunited companions sat on padded benches in a passenger compartment, rather like a partition inside the hull of a battleship. A small army of mercenaries were also packed in around them, chattering, but they had semi-privacy. Tina's mother and grandparents were with the driver in the cockpit.

Tina squirmed her way into the back seat, sitting between Jeremy and Maren, extending her arms behind their backs. "We have the *fancy* tank! Hors d'oeuvres?" A manservant approached and leaned across the bench, swaying as he held a fruit, cheese, and cracker platter in front of them.

Jeremy seized a cracker and cheese slice. "I need to see what's going on outside, I'm getting claustrophobic in here."

"There's a peep hole over there." Tina pulled a tablet out of her extravagant purse and flicked it on. "But check this out." The screen displayed a live feed from several cameras outside the tank. The streets were swarming with people carrying groceries. Fist fights were breaking out. The windows of stores and cars were smashed, and smoke poured out from a few overturned cars, strewn about Manhattan like children's toys. Other cars, gorged with supplies, tried to make their way through the crowds, but people were surrounding them and pounding on the windows. Gunshots cracked in the distance. The massive tank rumbled down the street, parting the seas.

Frisky stared at the screen in disgust. "I can't eat right now." She handed her grapes to Maren.

CHAPTER 11

THE HAMPTONS

Tina's place in the Hamptons had changed since Jeremy and Maren were last there. A twenty-foot-high barbed wire fence lined the perimeter of the four acre property, which had expanded to include several nearby lots. The foundations of what would be guard towers were in construction at regular intervals abutting the fence. The front lawn was ripped up and workers were busy laying down concrete. Much of the fancy landscaping was replaced by tanks, helicopters, and a few handsome jets. Several golf carts were lined up neatly next to Tina's house, a luxurious Victorian which seemed out of place now. A bulldozer was pushing debris which used to be a neighboring home. In a field to the west, a crane was lowering steel beams into a pit dug in the ground.

"We've sort of... acquired some things," said Tina.

"Your father's a man of vision," said Jeremy, as they exited the tank down the ramp.

Construction workers rushed past them, carrying orange safety cones and shouting at another group of newcomers. "Wet cement! Get off it!" Frisky jumped out of the way as a group of workers came towards her shouldering large sheets of plywood. "Tina, can you take us somewhere less hectic, please?"

"Follow me," she beckoned with a sexy finger. She led the party through her family's home. People were walking around the ground floor, and the place was full of Silicon Valley types tapping away at laptops, talking with soldiers and pilots. Tina's parents were standing at the redwood table in the former dining room, pointing to maps and talking with soldiers. Tina led them up the spiral staircase and into her princess bedroom. Jeremy nodded at the oil painting of Michael Jackson on the wall.

"We have lots of tents, and they're building bunkers too, but I insist you guys stay here." She opened her eyes wide and gasped. "Sleepover Part II!"

"Tina, I appreciate your attempt at establishing what I think is supposed to be a sense of normalcy, but can you tone it down a bit?" Frisky swatted a fly from her neck.

"Ew, how'd that get in here. I know, let's do makeovers!" They all laughed, but Tina was dead serious.

"Frumpy Frisk needs a facial."

An hour later, a great bell rang throughout the compound. Tina nearly poked Frisky's eye out with her eyeliner. "Eek! Speech time!"

Jeremy was admiring himself in a mirror, pleased with his exposed midriff in Tina's lime green tank top. He jumped when Maren shook his shoulders from behind.

"The bell beckons," she said.

Tina drew back the curtains.

The cement block just outside their window was still partitioned off with safety cones, but a line of people passed beside it on a black tarp that had been laid down to direct foot traffic. They were walking towards a makeshift wooden pavilion thirty yards away. "Must have let more people in from the outside. Is there even room for them here?" asked Frisky.

Tina shrugged. "Sure. Let's go."

Jeremy, Maren, Tina, and Frisky walked along the tarp-path and took a seat on the ground that had been cleared in front of the small wooden pavilion. Five rows of people separated them from the stage, where Tina's father stood barrel-chested and proud, holding a mic. A cluster of soldiers stood behind him with arms crossed, with one stooping low in front of an amp, adjusting the volume.

"Testing, testing," said Tina's father. He tapped the mic and then cleared his throat. "Hello, I'm General Grant Forero. Welcome to your new home, everyone. We'll be expanding the compound and securing the perimeter further out and right now we're looking at a square mile of safety. Bunkers are being built over to your left," he pointed, "and we're also busy working on a common area, which will go up right behind me. More structures will be built as our community grows. We're working twenty-four-seven. A big thanks to the men and women who've pooled their resources together to make this happen."

Everyone cheered.

"My work in aviation has taught me how useful it is to get a bird's eye view of things, so be sure to check out the guard towers which'll be up in the next month or so. You might even take a shift at watch." He pointed again. "It's a war zone out there, make no mistake about it. With the explosion in population, basic necessities will be scarce. The entire economy is crumbling, and law and order has broken down."

The crowd roared, and a big man with a thick neck stood up in the center of the dirt field and waved his arms around belligerently. Those beside him pulled him back down.

The General lifted his hand up. "We're going to rebuild a society, right here. The first priority is to secure these borders. We can't let more people in than we can support, unfortunately. From now on, no one is to leave the compound without authorization. If you do, I can't guarantee we'll let you back in. We have scouts further out, but in the off-chance that a group of outsiders make it to the fence, do not engage with them. All communication with those outside will be by a commanding officer." He held up a military uniform with a blue zigzag stitched across the chest. "This blue pattern on the jacket is our flag, so take note. We'll be hoisting one up shortly on that flag pole over there.

"We can only hope and pray that order is restored for the folks on the outside, as we give thanks for our own good fortune. On our last run into the city, one of my sources informed me that a catastrophic earthquake has destroyed much of southern California." General Forero paused and allowed a pregnant silence to fill the night air. "And not only that, but in Japan too, right near Fukushima. Chemical warfare has broken out in the Middle East. Every government is now rotting from the inside." The General slammed his fist into his hand. "But not here! So keep the spirit, folks. I'll speak to you all soon. And goodnight."

Jeremy and Maren made their bed in silence as they digested the news. Their room was large and inviting, with a Queen-sized bed, a dresser, a nightstand, and a small, round marble table in the corner. Two bright yellow benches were at either side of the table and Jeremy was content that Tina had not had a hand in the decorating. But no matter the warmth of their new home, the truth remained that their parents were out there, possibly in Japan or Iran, without shelter, food and water. Maren tucked the bed covers in snugly and then smoothed her hair down. "We can play house for a little bit, but soon you're going to have to answer your calling."

"I want to be incognito for a while, you know?"

"Why?"

Jeremy stared at her. "I'm not ready."

Maren gave him a small nod.

The next morning, Jeremy slept in.

Maren sat up in bed and attempted to brush her hair with her fingers. She discovered she had massive knots. "Ugh!" She tiptoed past Jeremy and went to go find Tina.

"Tina!" She rapped on Tina's bedroom door, but jumped when Tina tapped her from behind.

"Looking for me? Great! 'Cause I'm looking for you!"

"Have a brush?" Maren attempted to run a hand through her hair to demonstrate the severity of her problem. "Ren?!"

Tina motioned for Ren to step forward. The trusty young guard bowed to Maren, daughter of the family he'd served all those years.

"Oh my God, look at you!" Tina smacked Ren on the shoulder, interrupting his chivalry.

"How are you here?" asked Maren. "What happened to you?!"

"My parents and I went to sleep that night before we were to escape together—and then, well I came here. Not here, but close by. We were looking for you, and instead we found some soldiers who knew your names. Anyway, we were led to this compound."

"Well I'm glad to see you again!" Maren embraced Ren.

"See you later, Ren!" said Tina. She nudged him away. "Go see someone downstairs and they'll get you situated. Maren, shut up and talk to me!" Tina pulled Maren into her bedroom and slammed the door. "Who is that handsome man, tell me all about him and I want to eat dinner with him."

Maren crinkled her nose. "Get me a brush, first."

An hour later, and Maren was turning in front of the mirror. "Awesome," said Maren, stretching the purple zebra-print leotard down over her butt.

Tina clapped and laughed. "You're a good sport, Maren! You'll get your clothes back soon enough. You stink, girl."

Maren sighed and slipped her backpack on. They left Tina's room, walked down the winding Victorian stairs, and headed outside. They made their way to the back of the property, where there was a wooden bathhouse painted sky blue. Maren imagined that it must have been peaceful to wash here after a long day at the beach, but now, in times of Apocalypse, it had become a madhouse.

"Outta my way!" shouted Tina. "General's daughter coming through! Important business here." She yanked Maren forward. "You're going next. Just bring your clothes in the shower with you. I'll hang on to this."

"Oh, I can wait," said Maren sheepishly, but Tina was already unzipping the zebra printed leotard.

"Don't gawk at my girl," snapped Tina at a man behind her. "So does Ren like brunettes? Or is my hair black? More like dark brown."

Maren let out a little yelp and then Tina pushed her into the shower stall and pulled the curtains taut. The shower's previous occupant stumbled out, naked and confused.

"I don't know." Maren showered quickly. Tina helped her back into the leotard, much to Maren's annoyance. Wet, clean clothes in hand, the two set off back to the house.

The General's second in command, Thomas Blakely, halted Maren and Tina at the front door of the Victorian.

He was an older man, and looked more business than military. Tina nudged Maren. "He's my father's CFO," she grumbled.

"We've set up a work chart," said the man sternly. "Your father will be posting it by the gazebo, but I have a copy here." He held out a stack of papers and a digital camera to Tina. "We haven't gotten a proper census yet, and I think that will help things move along."

Tina rolled her eyes. "My dad is an OCD control freak."

"Tina, your father wants you to get pictures and background information from every resident. In addition to the background information, we want a first-hand description of every resident's personality. Don't take notes until after you've spoken with them, we don't want to arouse suspicion." He turned to Maren. "Tina's told us you have quite the memory, so use it."

"Well, our job sounds fun anyway!" Tina fist pumped.

An hour later, and Maren and Tina were in the barracks photographing residents. The barracks were rows of trailer homes, with wooden ramps and decks. Cots lined the walls of the trailers and room dividers provided minimal privacy.

"Name," said Tina flatly, already bored with her special job.

"Frederick Alister," replied a man whose thin black hair was parted purposefully to the side to suggest thickness.

"Here," Tina handed him a form to fill out while she took notes.

"Remember to rename the file on the camera this time," said Maren, looking over Tina's shoulder.

"Hey," said a warm voice from the doorway of the barracks. Jeremy posed, arms flexed dramatically while giving his best smolder-stare. "Take my picture?"

"Sure," said Maren, nodding to Tina with a wicked smile. Click.

"Excellent," she said, holding the camera up for all to see. "What an ass! Everyone only gets one picture, so this is kind of a forever moment."

"Wait." Jeremy reached out for the camera but Tina pulled it to her chest.

"Did you see your job assignment yet?" blurted Tina.

"Assignment?" Jeremy shook his head, then sighed. "Whatever it is, I'm game. I'm trying to blend in."

"Let's go check the jobs' bulletin." Tina waved goodbye to Frederick, and Maren and Jeremy followed her out of the barracks to the center of the compound.

"Jeremy Chikalto!" yelled Tina, setting her finger on the board.

"Wait, wait." Jeremy pushed her aside.

"Well—what's your job?" asked Maren.

Jeremy turned from the bulletin board, and his brows furrowed as a grave look spread across his face.

"Let me see." Maren stepped forward.

"Slop duty," said Jeremy, barely audible.

CHAPTER 12

ABANDON

Jeremy dragged his feet towards the makeshift log cabin that was serving as the slop supplies dispensary. It was a hastily built structure, probably not up to code, and likely to collapse if flicked. He was fifty feet from it when he felt something land on top of his head. "What?" Jeremy looked up and then was struck by a meaty piece of hail. "Ouch!" Pellets were falling from the sky. Then a large one the size of Jeremy's fist shattered just inches away from him.

Jeremy sprinted to the dispensary and took shelter inside. He shielded his brow and looked out across the lawn. People were running in every direction. *Maren.* No sooner had the thought crossed his mind, then Jeremy disappeared into the Haze and reappeared in the center of the compound. He ran up the steps of the small amphitheater past the bulletin board and looked out. "Maren!" he shouted. The Victorian wasn't far.

He ran out into the hail storm, allowing his body to generate a soft buzz of protection. The hail bounced off his shield and sizzled, and all around him the earth bore pot holes. He jogged across the cement pathway and then flickered inside the Victorian. "Maren!"

Maren was seated on the stairs, huddled together with Tina, Tina's mother, and two small children. And then as suddenly as the hail storm started, it ended.

Everyone waited in silence for a moment to see if it was really gone.

"That was... interesting," Tina managed.

"Let's find your parents." Tina's mother, Anna, led the two small children to another room.

Tina's father came barreling down the stairs. "Move. Move. Everyone, back to your posts!"

"Dad, no."

He held his hands up to her, ignoring Jeremy's scowl. "One little hail storm can't derail our operation here. We've probably incurred damage to our perimeter. Let's get moving, people. Tina, set a good example. I'm making an announcement." General Forero marched to the bottom of the stairs, out the door and towards the amphitheater.

"Intense father figure," said Jeremy.

"He's right, Jeremy. We of all people know how much worse it can be," said Maren. "We need to get this compound in order."

"I hardly think slop duty is a priority right now."

Maren snort-laughed, and then was embarrassed by her snort.

The General made his announcement over the loudspeaker, the bell was rung, and slowly everyone got to work. Jeremy, for his part, attempted slop duty. He was given a cart with two buckets, a mop, and a single pair of latex gloves. "I want the purple gloves," he snapped at the dispensary worker. There was one set of purple gloves and three pairs of yellow. The dispensary worker—an older woman with short, curly brown hair—smiled at him as she handed him the purple gloves. Jeremy snatched them up and straightened his posture. His breathing had become labored and everyone in the dispensary was beginning to stare.

Jeremy set the gloves on top of his cart, pulled a comb out of his pocket and began to comb his hair into a perfectly-tousled state.

"Move your cart to the slop deck," said the old woman in a droll voice.

Jeremy threw his comb onto the cart. "I will."

"Jesus Christ." A bald man with a wide chest rammed Jeremy's cart with his own, sending a bucket careening across the floor. The man laughed and a few onlookers joined in.

"A real slapstick crowd." Jeremy rolled his eyes and picked up the bucket. "I'm so above this." He pushed his cart out to the slop deck to receive his assignment.

Jeremy Chikalto—Barracks C and D

Like a cow herded to the slaughter, Jeremy pushed his cart forward. The warm sun beat down on his cheeks and he took a deep breath. Outside, young children were playing with the larger chunks of hail that hadn't melted while an elderly woman was hanging clothes on a line to dry. Two men in hard hats were pointing to the lookout tower under construction. Jeremy pushed his cart onward and then dallied for some time in front of an old van that had been converted into a small bakery. Plain, hard bread loaves were being distributed to a young couple. The woman—around Jeremy's age—wafted the scent of the fresh baked good past her nose.

"Slop duty," Jeremy uttered to himself. There was no way he could go through with this.

"Cajjez Jeremy!" It was Ren. He had jogged past Jeremy but was now jogging backwards. He slowed and waited for Jeremy to push the cart beside him.

"Hello, nice to see you again on the other side of the universe?" Jeremy cocked his head to the side.

"Long story. Some storm, right?" Ren stood with both hands on his hips and breathed in the cool air. "Miraculous, Cajjez, simply miraculous."

Jeremy nodded and looked up at the sky.

"On to your job, then? No time for digestion in this place. Probably good for me. I'm still in shock." A lump caught in Ren's throat. He leaned over Jeremy's bucket. It was empty. "What do they have you doing?"

Jeremy shook his head. "I can't do this."

"Well it couldn't be any worse than slop duty...." His voice trailed off. "They've got *you* on slop duty?" Ren drew back from Jeremy.

"Yes, damn it. I can't."

"Utterly unthinkable, Cajjez."

"I know!" Jeremy kicked his cart and it rolled forward slightly. "I think I'm done here, actually." Jeremy abandoned his cart.

"Hey." Maren tapped Jeremy on the shoulder. He had dozed off under a dead tree beside the big house.

Jeremy started up. "Everything okay?" He rubbed his eyes.

"I heard about your slop duty, and your unreturned cart." Maren sat down beside Jeremy. "While I do think it would do you some good to humble yourself—"

Jeremy gave a look of disgust.

Maren straightened. "I think you need to knock it off. That hail storm was weird, right? I'm surprised we didn't suffer any casualties." She dug her fingers into the dirt beside the tree and let it run through her hands. "You can travel through the Haze, Jeremy. Like it or not, this is the Apocalypse, and you're an angel. You need to explore the universe—the Haze—and find out more information, not sit here brooding over rubber gloves and buckets."

"I told you already—I'm not ready. But listen, I need you to cover for me."

"Why? For what?"

"I'm going to look for our parents. I'll be quick. Just going to check the Donegall Estate, maybe leave a note for them in case they seek it out. Makes sense, right? If everyone from the Farmoore Galaxy's been transported to Earth, they'll do their best to make it to that point, since it's where we first met, before..."

"Mantel's Maze, yes it makes sense." Maren sighed.

"So, later!" Jeremy vanished.

Jeremy was swimming in the Haze through a vast purple ocean. The spirit animals bobbed up and down aimlessly in the waves. Jeremy only had to twist his body slightly, dip into another fold in space, and then pop right out onto the Donegall Estate. The sensation of knowing a place from inside the Haze was more satisfying than being a steward of wine, and knowing the location of a particular house was his oak finish. Jeremy smiled as he felt the familiar zap and pull, and was about to twist his body around to exit the Haze, when his demons rushed around him.

He shrank back, but then remembered his power. "Leave me be," he said, pushing the demons out with his energy.

The demons were blown back, but they regrouped into a spiky line and began to undulate. Jeremy felt the waves come by, like he was waist deep in a black ocean, waiting for a good wave, and the water line was sharp and cut him in half. He watched the black swells crest, and the capes swayed on the surface like cobras.

The demon at the end of the line brushed back its shadowy hood. "Sequere me."

Jeremy swam forward into the waves, but then the demons stopped and the Haze was still and empty. Jeremy looked around, but the spirit animals were gone. Subconsciously, he swam into line with the demons. And then we was in them, swaying with the waves, but the demons rose up into a roaring wall, and crashed into him and he tumbled into sharp shells. All around him he saw the gaping "O" of their mouths and then he was dissolved, and he sank down with a hundred anchors into a sea of red until all was black again.

CHAPTER 13

HELLSCAPE

Jeremy was standing on parched earth split by a thousand fault lines, and each crevice glowed and spit embers. He stumbled forward, and his footsteps scattered sparks across the hellscape. In front of him was a dull gray smoke and an expansive emptiness, and he could feel the thumping of his heart against his chest. He blinked, and in that brief moment when his eyes were closed, he saw the faces of the dead pressing up into him, gruesome and intimate. He inhaled them and they screamed in his bones, a dissonant chorus of ten-thousand voices. Then he blinked and was back in the empty gray hellscape with the burning embers.

He had to blink again and saw horrible things in a rush, in his veins, threatening to explode his heart from the inside. He tried not to blink again. He walked forward, but his eyes were drying in the heat of the embers and felt like sandpaper. "Demons?"

He tried to cross over into the Haze, but there was a wall there. "Demons, take me out of here!"

He blinked and the dead snaked around him with stinking corpses. They pressed up against him, pushing a gelatinous substance into his mouth. The demons condensed in front of him between two of the bodies. The blood and innards filled up all of the spaces between the bodies and Jeremy was anchored down, and couldn't move. Worms and maggots bubbled in his ears. He called again for the demons, but his mouth was full of the gelatinous substance. Another demon flickered into his peripheral vision and approached him with an open "O" mouth. Jeremy wanted to go through it, to get back into the Haze, but he was paralyzed. He tried to will his demon to swallow him, but the demon closed the "O" of its mouth and leered at Jeremy.

Do I blink? Can I go back to the gray? His mouth was full of the sludge and he tried not to think about what it might be. *I can't go like this.* Jeremy tried to spit out the ooze and worked his tongue hard to push back against the slow tide of death. The leering demon flattened itself in the small space in front of Jeremy, smiled, and then it opened up its "O" mouth again.

Jeremy shoved his hand into his own mouth and began to claw at the gelatinous substance. He wished he would faint before he had to take his last breath, the breath that would kill him. He clawed harder and harder, and then gripped both hands around the base of his tongue. He pulled it out with his nails, severing it from its base, and held it in front of him. There was ooze, blood, and slime and suddenly he was in a pocket of air, beautiful air. He breathed and returned to the expansive hellscape.

Thunder shook the gray land and in the distance a great drum beat. It grew louder and closer. Ahead, the gray opened up and in the distance a bright orange flame blossomed, brighter than the sun. Jeremy's demons swirled around him, obscuring his view of the sun, and then the demons were gone.

Jeremy was leaning against the perimeter fence on the compound. He bent forward and coughed up blood onto the dirt. His mouth tingled for a second and he slid his tongue along the roof of his mouth. It was intact and the sensation of death was gone.

CHAPTER 14

CHEERS

Jeremy stumbled towards the Victorian house. His body had completely healed, but his mind was numb. Guard towers now circled the house, supporting a huge platform above the roof. Behind the jet field were three big greenhouses with people bustling inside, cultivating crops. Soldiers were doing drills all over the place. *How long have I been gone?*

General Forero rounded the corner, accompanied by three soldiers. They were wide men with impeccable postures and serious frowns.

"Hello there, son. I don't think we've had a good talk yet," said General Forero.

"Later," Jeremy shook his hand. "I have to find Maren."

General Forero exchanged a look with his second in command. "My daughter has told me strange things— excuses. You've shirked all of your responsibilities to date. Too good for slop duty, too tired for night watch, too weak of a stomach for the slaughter house. I haven't seen you in three weeks! I call bullshit. I put you up at my daughter's request, in my own home. I could transfer you to the barracks in a second. My soldiers want to know why the entitled little piss gets the nice room. Care to talk?"

Jeremy laughed and then slapped himself on the cheeks a few times. "I've been gone for three weeks?"

"My daughter's convinced you're some kind of royalty. I think you're nothing but a leech, so maybe she's right."

Jeremy rushed the General and gave him a hug, patting him on the back. "Your sneer is the same vertical line given to me by Tina following a bout of unrequited love."

General Forero leaned forward. "Do you have a death wish, boy?"

"I've been granted a second chance. But listen, my father was a stern man too, principled, he'd call it. I may not be. But what I've inherited is better—loyalty. I was out looking for my family and I won't be giving up on them, or anyone else I care about. You'd be wise to get in my favor. Now if you could please just move out of my way."

"Oh? I don't think I'll be doing that until I get some answers," said the General.

Jeremy glanced behind the General, eager to see Maren. "Your power is only a small fraction of mine. I could have you calling me Cajjez Jeremy in a second, if I wanted."

The General and his soldiers laughed. "You think you have power. I still consider you my daughter's kidnapper, a thief, stealing my jet. The only reason we're playing nice is because I love my daughter. I built a business empire and now an army. You know how many young fools have challenged me in my life? The world's going to shit, and I'm the only one who can clean it up. The world needs a leader, not some sniveling, selfish boy. You have built nothing. A kingdom was probably handed to you and you dropped it from your butterfingers. Either follow my rules, or be exiled for your insubordination."

"Tina, your daughter, bows to me. You should also know that I have more influence over her now than you do."

General Forero cocked his arm back like he was at bat, and slapped Jeremy across the face with the back of his hand, but Jeremy didn't flinch. "Do you like magic tricks?" A mischievous grin spread across Jeremy's face.

The General was about to finish his lecture, when Jeremy pulled a raccoon out of the air by its tail, and it began to screech and swat about. The soldiers and the General jumped a little bit, and Jeremy put it back behind the air.

There was a long silence. "Jacey Moon, they called you. Murderer," said General Forero in a low voice.

"I do prefer to think of myself as a magician, though. I can pull other things out of the air, things that would hunt you down like an animal." There were a few whispers in the air, coming from behind the perimeter fence, and the soldiers drew their guns and pointed them at the shadows, but the General stood fast.

"Right," said Jeremy. "And you can call me Cajjez from now on."

Jeremy was let inside the Victorian home and he was about to ascend the staircase when he heard a familiar voice call to him from the dining room.

"My son!" Vor Wantoro appeared, his hands firmly

planted on the back of Vinya Raaychila's wheelchair, smiling despite himself, a short cropped beard framing his square jaw. Raaychila was angelic in her chair, her red hair radiant in the soft light.

Jeremy laughed and then ran to them. He hugged his father and mother, then joyfully took his mother's hand and kissed it.

"Jeremy, old boy!" It was Mateo.

"Hello, Mr. Nononia," said Jeremy, jolly as a spring chick.

"Oh," Mateo shooed him away. "It's 'Mateo,' come on now."

"Are you okay?" asked Raaychila. "We were so worried. You look famished!"

"Someone get my son something to eat!" Wantoro called out. "We celebrate!"

"I suppose you should let Maren know you've returned," said Raaychila with a twinkle in her green eyes.

Jeremy nodded, bowed clumsily, and then raced up the stairs. He ran down the hallway and flung open his bedroom door.

There was a stirring under his bedcovers, and then the blankets pulled back revealing Maren and a shirtless Ren.

CHAPTER 15

LIGHT OF MINE

"Jeremy!" Maren sprang up.

"What are you doing?" stuttered Jeremy. He felt behind him for the door as the blood rushed to his head. "What the hell, Maren."

"Oh," Maren said, realizing how bad it looked. "Jeremy, I missed you so much!"

Ren climbed out of the bed and pointed to his watch. "My watch," he stammered.

"Yeah, it's time to get the fuck out." Jeremy flashed between them and faced Ren, his back to Maren. "Get out."

"Jeremy, he was just showing me his watch—it glows in the dark." Maren spoke in a small voice.

"It's got a solar battery and it doubles as a flashlight," said Rex.

Jeremy stared blankly at Rex. "I'll give you a solar powered fist if you don't get out."

"Jeremy, it's not what it looks like," said Maren.

Jeremy turned to her as Rex exited the room, shutting the door behind him. "So is this Mitch, the sequel? How could you possibly get under the covers with a guy who has a flashlight watch." He glared at her. "He was in my bed. His shirt was... missing!"

"Oh, it's not like that Jeremy." Maren reached out to him for a hug. "He spilled orange juice on it," she added.

"Whatever. I'm alive, you're alive, our parents are alive. Let's celebrate." Jeremy walked out of the room and slammed the door behind him.

Jeremy ran down the stairs and past the data crunchers huddled together over a large wooden table. He slipped between soldiers mapping out their next raid and entered the dining room. His mother and father smiled at him, and then Tina pushed her way through the small crowd and ran to him. She embraced him and he squeezed her back.

"I knew you'd come back!" she said, smiling up at him with brown, made-up eyes. Mascara dripped down her lashes and stained her cheeks charcoal, and she wiped the tears away with her sleeve.

"Crying for me?" said Jeremy. And then he cried a little too.

CHAPTER 16

IN GOOD COMPANY

Jeremy's friends and family spent the rest of the day celebrating the reunion. Jeremy kept a safe distance from Maren, but was pleasant enough and laughed freely. They sat in a garden for a time, and Wantoro regaled the party's adventures; only a minor hail storm derailed their fun for a few moments, but there'd been many hail storms in Jeremy's absence and people had come to accept them.

That night, after Jeremy's parents and Mateo had retired, Jeremy invited his friends back to his room, which was plenty spacious and accommodating for a crowd. The best feature was the cozy balcony. Jeremy waved Ren aside. "Ren, come out here." Jeremy slid open the glass door to the balcony. The air was damp and heavy. Jeremy took a deep breath and let the cold fill his lungs. He turned to Ren and gestured to the bottles kept on a small round table. "I'm glad this is here because I no longer plan to be just a casual drinker." He handed Ren a glass and poured him some scotch. "To miraculous reunions."

The two clinked glasses.

"So Maren discussed everything with you?" asked Ren. "We're good then, right?" He smiled and took a small sip of scotch.

"No." Jeremy stood up and Tina came out on the balcony, bumping into Jeremy with her hips. "I want to drink with you guys, too!" She began hopping up and down.

"I'll take something," said Frisky, poking her head outside. "But can we close the door? It's getting drafty."

With the door to the balcony once again shut, Jeremy and Maren's room was a warm and inviting space. It was a large room, but the way the furniture was arranged made it seem intimate. Jeremy dimmed the lights beside the nightstand, pulled back the curtains to the balcony, and allowed a soft moonlight to filter in. Then he stood up on his bed and waved the bottle of scotch.

"I'm so happy to be back. It's great we're all here together. And so strange—I only felt like I was gone for a second, but three weeks?" He whistled. "Wow, so much can change. Including the people you think you know best." Jeremy tipped the bottle back and took a long swig. Tina cheered.

"Can you finally tell us where you've been?" asked Maren. She smiled sweetly up at him.

"Where have I been," repeated Jeremy. "Sure, I can pull the blankets back and reveal my little secret." He winked at her, then took another swig. "I went to Hell."

Everyone quieted.

"Are you okay?" asked Tina, breaking the silence.

"I guess." He laughed. "I followed my demons. Came this close to eternal damnation," he pinched his thumb and pointer finger together. "Escaped with my life—dignity in tact, until, of course, I came back to a hell of a surprise."

Jeremy wagged his tongue crudely at his friends.

"Jeremy, you need to start drinking water." Maren reached up to him and grabbed his hand to lead him down. He recoiled from her.

"Oh, let him get wasted, Maren!" Tina gave Maren a gentle nudge. "Promise we'll all forgive him for his drunken shenanigans. He *earned* this!"

"I did, I think," said Jeremy. "Let's dance!" Jeremy sang like David Bowie.

Jeremy put on a Frank Sinatra record while Tina went out to find more alcohol. He held his hand out to Maren, and she accepted. Then he whipped her about for a minute, at last flinging her onto the bed.

"Like that?" he asked. Tina returned and Jeremy grabbed a bottle of gin from her stash. He removed the lid and took a swig, his eyes trained on Maren. "Bitch," he whispered between gulps.

Maren sighed and got off the bed. She walked over to Tina, who was dancing seductively for anybody who would watch. Jeremy disappeared onto the balcony with his gin.

Frisky and Ren sat in the back of the room on bright yellow benches positioned around a small marble table, taking in the music.

"I miss my dog the most," lamented Frisky. "It's a crazy world out there now. He ran off when I first left my place. Got scared."

"Oh, there are plenty of dogs out there. They're managing. What did he look like?"

Frisky stared wistfully at the ceiling. "A brown pitbull

mix, with a patch of white shaped like a heart around his eye."

"Hey," said Ren, smiling. "I saw him last night on patrol. He was all right."

"Oh, stop!" Frisky shook her head.

"A sweet boy he was?"

Frisky nodded.

"He'll find a companion then. Times like these, everyone can do with a companion. A sweet dog will find a sweet love." Ren sipped at his scotch while Frisky nodded thoughtfully.

Jeremy approached the table and stumbled slightly over a chair. "Get up."

Ren stood and held up his hands. "Hey, we're good."

"What's going on?" asked Frisky.

Jeremy punched Ren in the face.

CHAPTER 17

STRIPPED DOWN

"Let's take this party outside!" yelled Jeremy. He raised his arms up in victory.

"Jeremy!" Maren helped Ren up. "Apologize to Ren."

"Oh please. 'I just got a new flashlight watch, want to see it under the covers? Oh, how inconvenient, I just spilled orange juice on my shirt. Better go check out that watch before Jeremy gets back.'" Jeremy pulled up his shirt to reveal his chiseled abs. "Like that, girls? I can share so much more. Come outside." Jeremy laughed and then took another swig. "I'm going to show you how we do it at the Donegall Estate."

"No, someone help me." Maren tried to steady Jeremy with her hand, but he disappeared and reappeared on the other side of the room.

"You don't get a say," said Jeremy, slurring his words. He walked out of the room.

It was dark outside. "Free show for the ladies and gentlemen!" yelled Jeremy, waving his arms overhead. "Everyone, come on down to the stage! Don't want to miss this!" A few lights flickered on in the bedroom windows of the bunkers. Jeremy aimed his palm at a lone tree that stood ten feet from the amphitheater. He shot a bolt of lightning at the tree and it went up into flames. "Oops!"

People were now pooling into the area surrounding the amphitheater to investigate the ruckus, many still in their bed clothes.

"Got to resurrect this dinosaur," said Jeremy, and he flicked on the amphitheater's sound system and looked through a stack of cds. He put one in and the speakers started to bump with a jungle drum and bass. Jeremy downed the rest of his beer and then stumbled to center stage. "Hey, here comes Maren and Ren! I need lighting— Ren, light me up with that flashlight watch!" Jeremy struck a pose, illuminated by the burning tree. He threw his empty beer bottle off the stage.

Jeremy's muscle memory pulled through and his feet began to two-step in time with the music. The bass pulsed through him and he rolled waves from his hips to his neck while unbuttoning his shirt. A few women cheered; men began to shout obscenities.

Jeremy ripped his shirt off and then spun around, using a free-standing pillar as a dance pole. He flipped around it gracefully, and then played with his pants. "I want a girl up here."

Maren was crying and Tina tried to comfort her but kept glancing at the stage. Jeremy pointed to Maren and eased himself down into a perfect split.

"Come on up, sweetheart."

"Stop," said Maren.

"Okay, not you, maybe you." Jeremy pointed to a tall young woman with shiny, mid-length brown hair. She giggled and then her friends pushed her forward. Jeremy helped her up to the stage. He danced for her and goaded her to help him take off his pants. Soon he was stripped down to a purple g-string.

Tina nearly died. "Maren, does he wear that under there all the time?!"

"No! This is so embarrassing!" Maren ran off and Frisky ran after her. Tina stole a final glance and then chased after them.

Jeremy continued to dance around, amusing the crowd with one-armed pushups and gyrating hips.

"Jeremy Chikalto, get off of that stage right now!" Raaychila rolled forward in her wheelchair and parted the crowd. Everyone quieted. Jeremy stumbled forward.

"Oh my God, mom—don't look!" Jeremy crossed his hands over himself and ducked low.

The crowd started to laugh and cheer.

"Jeremy, you listen to me. Get off that stage and put your clothes on."

"Soon!" Jeremy wiped the sweat off his brow, vomited and then lay down on the stage, passing out face-down on the wooden boards, butt cheeks exposed to the world.

CHAPTER 18

TO THE SKY

After being returned to his bed, Jeremy slept well into the following afternoon. Maren had moved into Frisky's room and waited patiently for Jeremy to awake so she could get some of her stuff. At around 2:00 pm, Jeremy slipped out of his room to grab a bite to eat, and Maren ran in to retrieve her brush and clothes. When Jeremy returned, he remained in his room for the rest of the day, save a few carefully orchestrated trips to the bathroom.

The next day, Jeremy ventured downstairs for dinner. People snickered as he passed.

"Hi," he mumbled to his father, taking a seat beside him.

"Hello," said Wantoro. He passed his son the orange juice. "You are a fool."

"Yeah, it was just a joke that no one got." Jeremy cleared his throat and watched as his mom rolled into the room. He shrank a little in his seat.

"I've washed your clothes, so you can come by my room to pick them up whenever."

"Yep," Jeremy rose from the table, grabbed his bowl of stew and juice, and quickly exited the room.

Maren was at the landing to the staircase.

Jeremy sighed and tried to walk past her, but then stopped short in front of her. "I hope you're enjoying this," he said cooly.

"I'm not," she replied. "Ready to join us mortals again, your grace?"

"You realize we're done, right?"

"What? I realize you're incredibly immature and reckless."

Frisky, who was making her way down the stairs with her hiking backpack on, leaned in, "I sort of realized that when he dropped acid and crashed a jet." She gave Jeremy a cursory grin. "But I hear you're in excellent shape, so keep up the good work." She let herself outside.

"Excuse me." Jeremy continued up the stairs.

It was nearing dusk and growing chilly. "It should have been here by now," said General Forero, pacing the lot in front of the main gate to the compound. The days were getting shorter and the nights were getting colder. They needed fuel and supplies. A soldier approached the General with his head bowed.

"The tank's been overrun by outsiders. We lost it, sir."

The General cursed. "Well, then we'll just have to send out another one. Our people need supplies." He looked around at his soldiers, but no one volunteered.

"General Forero, with all due respect, I suggest we wait."

"And what, let the red army find us and starve us out? Cut off our supplies? We need to be ahead of the game."

"They don't have our location," said the shortest soldier.

One of the soldiers cleared his throat and everyone turned in his direction. "They've taken some of our men as prisoners. They'll beat the location out of them. I think they'll be coming tonight."

It was the middle of the night when Maren awoke to the sound of Tina tapping on the bedroom door. Maren rubbed her eyes and sat up, mindful not to disturb Frisky. She tiptoed to the door and cracked it open.

"Hey," whispered Tina. "Something's up."

Maren slipped out the door and into the hallway. "What's wrong?" She gently closed the door behind her.

"If you look out the window in the front, you'll see." Tina grabbed Maren's hand and led her to a large bay window. She pulled back the curtains and sure enough, the soldiers were lined up in neat rows.

"A drill," said Maren.

Then the tanks' engines roared to life and rolled into position.

"I don't think so."

Across the large cement slab that separated the Victorian house from the front of the camp, the bedroom lights in the soldiers' barracks had turned on. Maren shrank back from the windows. Jeremy appeared behind her and looked out the window. A man was running towards the entrance of the base and the soldiers opened the gate.

The runner was shouting. A large blast shook the foundation of the house, and Jeremy, Maren, and Tina fell over. They scrambled to their feet and looked outside again. A swarm of soldiers from outside the base was pushing against the barbed wire fence. Those on the front line screamed as the barbs tore into their flesh, but the mass behind them just kept pushing. Grenades were launched over the fence, and again the ground shook.

"I'm getting my parents," said Jeremy. Jeremy was at his parents door in a flash, while the others ran after him. Jeremy pounded on the door.

A second later, Wantoro flung it open. "What's going on?"

"Jeremy?" Raaychila was already seated in her wheelchair and wheeled forward. "Is there nowhere else to go?"

"I want everyone in the next house behind us." Jeremy steadied himself on his mom's wheelchair as the house shook. "We're probably surrounded on all sides so the center of the compound is best, for now. Maren, get Mateo. Tina, get your mom and Frisky. Bring anyone you want to save here now and I'll move us back through the Haze. Quick!"

Maren and Tina ran off down the hallway and returned with their families. A bullet shattered the window just beside Jeremy and he reached around part of the group. He pulled everyone he could touch through the Haze and back out a hundred yards back, in the communal room of the low level military housing complex. Jeremy returned to the Victorian house and retrieved the second half of the group. A few stray residents had lingered into the room, and Jeremy felt compelled to make a third trip. Once everyone had assembled in the now crowded communal room of the housing complex, they bunkered down. All of the furniture was piled high around them. Jeremy slid down onto the floor, his back resting against a toppled black sofa.

"What the hell is going on out there?" asked Jeremy.

"Who are we shooting at?" Maren reached out towards Frisky.

"Starving civilians, our friends." said Frisky. "I knew this day would come. We're hoarding all the supplies. Things have to change."

Jeremy swatted at his skin. It was crawling. "I should do something, right?"

"Yes." Maren leaned forward. He could feel her breath on his neck. "Jeremy, you have to get the armies to disperse. Show them your demons."

Jeremy's heart pounded in his chest. He could end this, right now. He could step up and be whoever it was he was supposed to be. But the last time he'd seen his demons was still heavy on his mind. Had his demons betrayed him? Had they brought him to Hell?

The blasts outside were getting louder. Smoke was beginning to pour into the building.

Jeremy stood up. He had to do something. "Demons." It was all happening so fast. *I am not the Antichrist.* He held his hands up and the air vibrated. Slowly, an inky blackness collected and began to take shape. Red eyes glowed in the cloud.

Jeremy heard screaming below him as he rose up in

the air and disappeared from that place. He was in the sky now, leading his demons like the first bird in a flock. Jeremy flickered in and out of the Haze like the frames of an old-time movie. Smoke from the battle filled the air. For a second the fire ceased and there was a commotion of voices. Then the artillery turned on Jeremy and his demons. The night sky lit up with streaks of orange. A bullet ripped through Jeremy's chest and he fell from the sky like a falcon diving towards the Earth. But the Haze pulled him in and he quickly healed, emerging once more to hover in Earth's atmosphere. He crackled with electricity and formed a blue globe around himself. It hummed with power as he hovered closer to the ground, deflecting the bullets as he pressed onwards, weaving in and out of the Haze towards the civilian army. They were running from him—his plan was working. But then people started to fall in the fleeing crowd.

"No!" He hadn't meant to cause a stampede, but people were already being trampled. A demon floated beside him like a trusted steed egging him on to battle. Jeremy looked at it and saw that it felt nothing. "Tell me demon, have I saved lives just now? Have I?!" Jeremy pulled through the Haze and drifted upwards to take in a bird's eye view of the aftermath of his demon debut. What was left of the outsider soldiers had dispersed, and only General Forero's own army fired intermittently at the sky.

Jeremy willed his demons to stay in the Haze, and he rushed downwards, towards the trampled bodies. He lifted one up, then another, and pulled them through the Haze and into the common room. "Somebody help these people!" Jeremy's father ran forward.

Jeremy felt sick over the carnage, but he and his family were safe.

CHAPTER 19

NEW TASK

"Is everyone okay in here? Don't go outside!" A head popped into the common room, nodded, and then disappeared again. General Forero's soldiers were visiting all of the living quarters to calm the anxious citizens, but everyone would hear of Jeremy's demons soon. He only hoped no one recognized him as the angel leading the horde. His own group—aside from the few unknowns who he'd saved—knew to keep quiet. Jeremy turned to a woman and a man he'd saved. They were wedged in between a chair and a table, staring back at him with wide eyes.

"Listen," said Jeremy. "What you saw—"

The two stumbled to their feet and ran to the door, toppling a chair and causing a small avalanche of furniture. Jeremy didn't even bother to pursue them. "Everyone will deny whatever they say."

Everyone nodded quietly. Seeing Jeremy's demons was not easy, even for those who knew he was their master.

Daylight soon filtered into the common room. General Forero appeared in the doorway. "Jeremy Chikalto, can I have a word?"

"Daddy, please!" Tina leapt to her feet. "Get your goons out of here." She shooed away the men who shadowed him, and General Forero relented.

The men filed out and General Forero approached the group. He nodded at Wantoro, who had stood to his full height and crossed his arms. General Forero approached the Cajjez.

"I guess you've put it all together now, after your daughter's told you everything. How clever of you."

The General ignored Jeremy's taunt. "You scared the invaders off, and I'm grateful for that. But..." he trailed off.

"Yes?" Jeremy leaned in and smiled.

"What are you?" His voice was flat.

"Daddy, I told you!" Tina stepped in front of Jeremy and crossed her arms. "He's an angel."

"No angel leads a flock of monsters like that." The General was shaking. "Tina, come with me."

"She's with me," said Jeremy. "And you're with me too, or you're against me. Tell everyone that there's some simple explanation for what they saw. A drone, I don't know."

The General stared for a time, considering.

"You want mass hysteria on your hands? If you don't smooth this over, we're going to have a problem." Jeremy felt Maren's hand on his shoulder. "Let me help you. I'll get you supplies."

"Jeremy, just be honest with everyone," said Maren.

Jeremy glared at her.

The General opened his mouth to reply and Jeremy disappeared into the Haze and reappeared in the corner of the common room ten feet behind the General. "I can disappear and reappear wherever I want. Let me use my powers to get you supplies," he said.

General Forero jumped. "Okay," he said when he recovered. "Okay," he repeated weakly.

The group made their way back to the Victorian house and joined in the clean-up effort. Ren and Frisky accompanied the explosives unit and combed the area for undetonated grenades and shells. Maren cleared the glass and debris from shattered windows and damaged buildings. Tina volunteered to bandage up the wounded. But help was limited, as most of the residents cowered indoors, whispering to one another about the demons in the sky.

It was mid-day after the attack when the General came to Jeremy's quarters. He knocked on the door and Jeremy opened it.

"We need more medical supplies, mainly antibiotics and bandages. I've brought Sergeant Webbers here to give you a list of locations. I'm sorry there's no time for a... pause." General Forero pushed the door wide open and beside him stood Sergeant Webbers, who grunted.

Jeremy cleared his throat in response. He walked out into the hallway.

"You're going to want to try Dr. Tomerson's place first in Stony Brook, Connecticut. You should be able to do a night run. Dr. Tomerson's got three thousand under his command. But you'll have to go through Queens." Sergeant Webber's eye's darted to General Forero.

Jeremy wouldn't be going through Queens, but Sergeant Webbers didn't know about that.

"You sure you don't want him to at least take a helicopter? We've lost a lot of our—"

"I told you that he's very highly trained," snapped General Forero. "Best in his class at a special operations youth academy. Just tell him where the supplies are."

"Youth." Jeremy snorted.

Sergeant Webbers looked at the young man he thought he was sending to certain death. "Ten Asclepius Drive, the large blue hospital, on the basement floor. There's a back entrance that takes you to the Emergency Room. The place is heavily guarded. How many are going with you?"

General Forero held his hand up. "I'm sorry, Sergeant Webbers, but that's confidential information. Jeremy will take it from here. Hand over all of your intelligence reports and consider yourself excused from your duties. Jeremy will be getting your office."

Jeremy walked towards the Intelligence Office and met Tina halfway.

"Hey sexy," she said, stifling a laugh. "Going to the super-secret, psuedo-FBI Office? Or whatever. Just behind here," she pointed. The office was behind the military barracks in a single story brick structure.

"Thanks," said Jeremy, and he hastened his pace.

Tina jogged after him. "Do you want to talk about what happened?"

Jeremy slowed his pace. "About the demons, or about my stripping?"

"You looked amazing, trust me. There are some pictures circulating, very easy on the eye." She smiled.

"Of course that's what you wanted to talk about."

"Maren is pissed. Anyway, I think Ren's interested in Frisky."

They continued towards the office, at last reaching the front door. Jeremy dug his hands into his pockets and rolled on his feet. "You think I did the right thing, unleashing the demons?"

"Yes," said Tina. "You're in control. You'll use them for good." She opened the door.

Inside, the place smelled of building materials and a cold draft filtered in through the cracks around the door. Jeremy frowned at the hastily built structure, minimal furnishings and the general lack of tasteful artwork, but then again, a few trips to some art galleries and the place would be habitable.

"I can make this work." Jeremy gestured around him and patted the wall. "I'll put a hanging fern right here."

"Okay," said Tina softly. "Be safe."

Chapter 20

Invasion

Jeremy wasn't familiar with Connecticut, but Sergeant Webber's maps proved useful. He pulled out of the Haze near the Donegall Estate in Manhattan to try to orient himself north. The gates around the property had been scrapped and the house itself had been gutted. He barely recognized his former home. Car parts littered the streets. All the store fronts had been broken into. Jeremy gave a cursory glance around, and then squinted at the map.

"Look here." A male voice called out from inside one of the ransacked stores, but the speaker was hidden. "Tryin' to get killed, boy?" He laughed.

Jeremy stuffed his map back into his pocket and turned to the voice. "I'm not really worried about you killing me. Just point me in the direction of Columbia University, please."

"Some kind of smart ass?"

Jeremy took a step towards the store. An emaciated rat scuttled across his foot and he jumped. "Nevermind that. I just need to go north. Where's Connecticut, do you know?"

"Ya lookin' for the doc, smart ass?"

"Dr. Tomerson—"

"You'll be dead before they let you join 'em."

"How do you know?"

The man laughed. "Know anything about cannibalism?"

Jeremy ignored him and tried to make sense of the store fronts.

"If I'm in front of the Donegall Estate, then that should have been the deli. This subway would be the southbound entrance, so..." Jeremy pulled his map back out of his pocket and started to cross the street. With so many buildings leveled, Manhattan was an unrecognizable wasteland.

"Hey," called the familiar voice from behind him. A large man in a gray hoodie and matching gray cargo pants emerged from the rubble. Large clumps of brown greasy hair shot out from his hood. He smiled and Jeremy saw that a tooth was missing. The man blended in well with the environment. "I'm not done with you yet. Give me that map."

Jeremy stopped. "Nope."

"Give me the map." The man raised a pistol and pointed it at Jeremy.

Jeremy raised his hands in surrender. "Poof." He smiled at the man and then disappeared back into the Haze.

Jeremy shuddered in the purple ocean, but not because of all of the demons circling him like sharks. Was the man in gray a cannibal? What about the residents at Dr. Tomerson's compound? He felt something wet press against his heel. He recoiled at the sudden dampness, but sighed with relief when he saw that it was Lyrna pressing her nose into him.

"Meow."

"Still no dead coming through?"

"No." Lyrna bobbed up and down on a purple ray of light.

"It's not like people aren't dying."

"Bring dead into Haze?"

Jeremy scratched his head and grimaced. "Maybe? I'll see what I can do. In the meantime, I have to find this doctor."

"Meow."

Jeremy popped out again and was delighted to see a road sign that read, "Stony Brook - 10 miles."

It only took two brief whirls in and out of the Haze to land Jeremy inside Dr. Tomerson's compound. The hospital loomed large on one side of the street and on the other sat one-story medical buildings, which had apparently been converted into housing. A laundry line stretched from the Ear, Nose and Sinus Center to the E&M Radiology. A young woman tugged a t-shirt and jeans from off the clothesline. Just beyond the medical buildings stood a tall barbed-wire perimeter fence, similar to the one at General Forero's compound.

"Excuse me, can I offer my assistance?"

"Huh?" Jeremy turned to the voice. It belonged to an older man with a neat comb-over.

"Where are you supposed to be?" The man lifted up a notepad.

"Um, just going to get my clothes."

"Okay," said the man slowly. "And your name is?"

Jeremy ducked out into the Haze and reappeared around the side of the hospital. He needed antibiotics. Jeremy looked around at the tree branches, and then at a pointed rock. "Too dull." He walked to the side of the building and found a drain pipe. Jeremy slid down to the ground and gripped the pipe. He fired a surgical stream of energy onto it, cutting the end into jagged spikes, and the shower of sparks attracted some nearby attention. A police officer crossed the street towards him. Jeremy ducked down a side street.

"Stop!" yelled the officer, and Jeremy knew he was being chased.

After Jeremy turned a corner, he disappeared back into the Haze and then reappeared on the opposite side of the hospital. He lifted up the metal drainage pipe and turned the sharp end towards his skin. Jeremy ripped it down his arm and blood squirted onto the pavement. Still, the wound looked too clean. Jeremy grabbed some dirt and rocks and rubbed it into the wound, wincing. His arm throbbed. Jeremy raked the ragged edge of the drain pipe over his arm again and again, shredding his skin until it was unrecognizable. The pain made him glow blue and crackle with electricity. "Ah!" He concentrated on his breathing. Slowly, the glow faded and, trembling, Jeremy hobbled into the emergency room. "Help!" he called out. "I'm bleeding pretty bad here!"

A nurse ran to him from down the corridor. "What happened? What's your name?"

"Apollyon," he blurted out. He immediately wanted to take it back.

"Excuse me?"

"Is it bad? Am I going to lose it?" Jeremy tried to seem as frantic as possible and pulled his shredded arm to his chest. But the loss of blood was real and Jeremy was beginning to feel it. "I'm going to faint."

"We'll just be up here." The nurse placed a hand on his back and led him further down the hallway, but then stopped. "And, I hate to ask, but what's you're assignment?"

Jeremy couldn't take it much longer and grabbed the nurse and pulled her into the Haze with him. He stared down at his arm and watched it heal, the blood and grime dissolving into the Haze. But the spirit animals were stalking towards him, eyeing up the woman. His demons, too, drew close to the life-force. Jeremy pulled the nurse out from the Haze and sat with her in an empty room. "Hello," he greeted her when her eyes fluttered open.

She slid away from him on the floor. "What happened?"

"I'll tell you what's going to happen. You're going to show me where you keep the antibiotics."

The nurse's eyes widened as she tried to make sense of recent events. "But—your arm!" She gasped at the sight of his healed flesh.

"Yes, I know. But where do you keep the antibiotics." Jeremy was growing impatient.

"I can't tell you that. What is your assignment?"

Jeremy palmed his forehead. Why do people insist on the hard way? "Lady, I don't belong here. I'm a thief. I've come from outside your walls, and I'm going to steal some antibiotics." He frowned; his presentation was all off.

The nurse scrambled to her feet. "Just let me go, please." The nurse reached for the door, apparently about to let herself go.

Jeremy ran over and slammed his hand on the door to keep it sealed. "Consider this a hostage situation."

"If I tell you where the antibiotics are, will you let me go?"

"You'll tell me the wrong location, so no."

"Are you going to hurt me?"

Jeremy's dance wasn't going anywhere, so he decided to escalate things. "Appear, demons." A circle of dark figures appeared around Jeremy and his hostage. She screamed and crumpled into the fetal position on the floor.

"I control these demons. Tell me where the antibiotics are or I'll have them rip you to pieces." Jeremy strained to keep his words and his will separate, lest the demons act on his empty threat. "I'll know if you're telling the truth."

The woman was wailing now between irregular breaths. Jeremy leaned in. "I'll let you go if you tell me where the antibiotics are."

"They're down the hallway! There's a storage closet on the left—the light should be on! There'll be guards! Please let me live!"

"There won't be guards, trust me." Jeremy stepped over the woman and walked out into the hallway. He was met by a wall of running guards. They lifted their guns to him, but Jeremy simply willed a wall of demons forward and the guards broke ranks, a few firing a shot before they scurried away. Soon the hallway was empty. Jeremy jogged over to an unmarked door. The light was on. He opened it and stared in wonderment at all the shelves, intricately organized yet completely foreign in content. He began to read the labels on the medicine containers until he recognized one. "Amoxicillin, perfect." Jeremy swiped an armful and then tossed them behind the air and into the Haze. He hesitated for a second and then began tossing medicine at random into the Haze. The other side of the room had gauzes and medical tape, so Jeremy availed himself of the opportunity. That's when he heard a whimper. He stopped and looked around.

The whimper stopped briefly, but he had already spotted the pharmacist's shoe poking out of a large cabinet.

"Hey, it's okay, I'm not going to hurt you," said Jeremy.

"I'm sorry," said the man. "I'm sorry about your people."

His people were doing pretty well. Supplies were just running low. "Thanks," said Jeremy. "I'm sorry about... your people too. If there's anything you need, like a specific type of sandwich or shoes or something?" Jeremy cringed at his words.

A siren rang loudly throughout the compound. Jeremy and the pharmacist covered their ears. Jeremy looked out the window. "I guess that's my cue." But he could see now that the siren wasn't meant for him. The fence had been breeched. The side behind the Ear, Nose and Throat residence had been flattened and an army was running through the compound. In the daylight, the invaders looked like ghouls, gaunt with sallow skin and tattered clothes. Behind the front line were families, mothers carrying babies. Jeremy withdrew from the window. But a new round of shots made him leap up again. "What are they doing?"

"Oh God, they're here!" cried the pharmacist.

Without thinking, Jeremy pulled through into the Haze and then wove in and out of the sky above the army, just as he had back at his own compound. He emitted a brilliant aura.

"Listen to me!" he bellowed.

The shots trailed off, and there was screaming and crying. Then everyone cowered. A pregnant silence followed.

"You will all stop this senseless death. Whatever you need, I can provide it. Food for the hungry. Medicine for the sick." Jeremy allowed a blue light to emanate from his eyes. "Don't hurt these innocent children." He hovered to the ground, flickering in and out of the Haze, the air crackling, and the crowd parted before him. He landed softly and walked to a woman cradling a toddler. "What do you need?"

She cried and hugged the child. "I need food."

Jeremy squatted beside the woman and brushed his hand across the girl's face. He disappeared into the Haze, and the crowd murmured. A minute went by, and people were shouting now. But then Jeremy flashed into sight again, and everyone was quiet. He handed the small child a plum, which she began to devour.

Jeremy found the power in his voice. "Follow me, and I will provide what you need. You are all brothers and sisters now, and a man who kills his brother will be exiled."

Then he pulled through to the hospital and broke into a vending machine, spilling its contents out onto the floor. He grabbed a nearby tray, scooped up the snacks, and then reappeared outside. "Here," he said handing the woman cookies, two fruit grain bars and two water bottles. "And here," he turned to a father and his daughter and handed them crackers, fig bars, and a soda. Jeremy continued to place food and drink into the now outstretched hands until he ran out. "If anyone spills a drop of blood while I'm gone, they'll answer to me." He crackled in emphasis. "Be patient."

Jeremy went back and forth into the barracks, feeding those with outstretched hands, raiding the pantries of houses, until the dark of night crept into the sky. But his work wasn't done. He gathered his constituents together.

"From now on, you'll all be responsible for more people. Family will be paired with family, and they are your new charges." And he went into the people and paired the strong with the weak, so that the whole of every group was greater than the sum of its parts. Then they all took an oath that they would protect their new siblings.

Jeremy arrived exhausted back at General Forero's compound, to find Maren waiting up for him. She was sitting out on their balcony, her keen eyes set on the gate at the front of the compound. Jeremy sighed then tapped her on the shoulder.

"Hey," she said. She pulled her legs to her chest and wrapped her arms around herself.

"It's pretty bad out there." Jeremy drummed his fingers on the table. "People need my help. If I could just harmonize this one microcosm, maybe the rest of the world will follow." He straightened. "Get your ass out of here, Maren, before I spank it."

"I thought you might want to talk." Maren frowned. "You're despicable." She left him alone on the balcony.

CHAPTER 21

CONSUMING

Jeremy spent the next few days at Dr. Tomerson's compound.

Maren splashed water on her face. It was getting dark out and Jeremy still wasn't home.

Frisky and Tina barged into her room and dragged her out. "Still moping? He'll come when he comes. But we found mint leaves!" Frisky led Maren outside and Tina followed, calling out to anyone who would listen. "Mint tea, bitches!"

They followed the cement path past the bunkers and then veered off towards the wooded area of the compound. There, the perimeter fence had just been pushed further out, and orange flags marked the newly conquered territory. Soon, the trees would be cleared. Patches of green, lush mint leaves grew in small clusters at the base of the fence.

Maren crouched down to inspect the leaves.

"It's tea time." Tina ripped up the plant.

"What are the medicinal properties of mint leaves?" asked Maren.

"Mint's fine." Frisky handed Maren a small container.

"Yeah, but I mean..." Maren sighed.

"Did you hear that?" Tina pointed just outside the perimeter fence. A stick snapped somewhere close, in the gloom. There were crickets.

Maren jumped. "Let's head back in."

"It's fine. What were you saying?" Tina smushed the leaves up against her nose. "This is great."

"I think I'm pregnant."

Tina gasped and inhaled some of the mint leaves into her mouth. She began to cough.

"Really?" asked Frisky. "When...?"

"Um, don't be naive, Frisk." Tina smiled and then spit up a mint leave.

Maren stood up. "There's someone out there." She pointed to the trees beyond the perimeter fence.

Tina wandered along the fence and then dropped into the tall weeds.

"What is she doing now?" asked Frisky. "Tina, get back here!"

"Head back," said Tina's voice in the weeds. "I'm talking to them."

Maren took a couple of steps back, but kept looking for Tina. A small flame alighted by the perimeter fence. A hand gripped her from behind and she screamed. Another hand covered her mouth. She was pulled to the ground and ropes bound her arms behind her. She gnashed her teeth and screamed out, but was gagged with a cloth. Tina was flung beside her. Her eyes were wide but she remained quiet. A group of strangers had infiltrated the camp and were circling them. Two tall, gangly men and three women with weather-worn faces stared down at them. They wore necklaces strung with teeth.

"Want to know a secret?" said a gaunt older man. His cheek bones jutted out and his lips were stained red. "Your friend looks delicious. What's her name?"

Maren wriggled but stopped as soon as she saw the boot stomp right in front of her belly.

"Her name is Maren."

"They feeding you well here, Maren? We know a source of endless food."

Maren tried to push the cloth out of her mouth with her tongue.

"She's pregnant," blurted Tina.

The man smiled and his teeth, like his lips, were bloodstained. "Maren, you ladies want to join us for dinner?"

A woman with stringy black hair in her face drew close to Maren and sniffed. Her teeth necklace brushed against Maren's chest. "To join us, one of you will eat the other. But it'll be okay!" The woman licked her lips and laughed. "Who will pass the test?"

A man grabbed Tina by the hair and brought her head down to the ground. She screamed and a boot kicked her head. She slumped forward and went limp.

Maren shook her head and pleaded with tears.

The old man grinned. "I'm going to take this rag out of your mouth and you just be quiet as a little church mouse. I'm going to cut my mouse a piece of cheese to eat." The man's eyes lit up, and he plunged a small knife into Tina's shoulder. She jerked up, and the pack of strangers fell on her like dogs. Just then Frisky leapt forward from behind a line of trees and shouted, and the hungry pack turned to a more lively sport.

From the behind the line of trees, Wantoro and Mateo emerged running, wielding a machete and a cast-iron frying pan respectively, and Ren was bringing up the rear with his sword. Frisky drew a hunting knife, cut Maren free from her restraints, and then joined in the charge. The strangers beat a hasty retreat, trying to take dinner with them, but someone dropped Tina in the weeds. The strangers scraped and tore their way under the hole in the barbed wire fence and fled into the night. A few johnny-come-lately soldiers ran to the fence and fired off rounds in the dark.

Chapter 22

Minor Key

Tina was brought to the medical ward—a neighboring house absorbed into the compound, stripped of unnecessary furniture and appliances, and painted a sterile white—and Maren excused herself to her bedroom over Frisky's protest. Maren shook violently, her nerves still splintered. The worst part about it was being silenced—she was sick of being gagged and bound, and considered herself an agent of change. A small part of Maren raged. She held her belly, which now seemed a foreign weight to her, and lay on her side.

"Hey," Jeremy appeared at the door. "Is Frisky here?"

"No."

Jeremy entered the room and sat on the sofa. "You look cute." He reclined and set his hands behind his head. "Want to come over here?"

"No."

"Everything okay?"

"Something happened."

"Yeah?" Jeremy frowned and waited expectantly.

Maren began to shiver again. "I'll tell you later." She couldn't bring herself to relive the fear she felt moments earlier. She'd almost lost the child she only just realized she carried. "I need to sleep."

"Okay." Jeremy lingered for a few seconds, and then left.

Maren dreamt that Jeremy was playing the piano and singing:

> The icicle shivers on the branch,
> Because the twig sprang up some new leaf-grass.
> All the time the moon sings,
> The sun bleats on its morning song.
> The world spun and a second moon answered.
> And I found you, Goddess.

The next morning, song birds gathered on the barbed wire fence and seemed to echo back Jeremy's song—only in minor key. Maren awoke with a jolt, half-expecting to find Jeremy beside her. But she was alone.

CHAPTER 23

IN PASSING

Following the cannibal attack, General Forero recruited more guards to work in shifts twenty-four hours a day walking the perimeter.

Maren visited Tina in the hospital.

"Dork, tell someone you need more rations! You got a friggin' angel baby growing inside you!" said Tina.

"Sshh, keep it down. I'll tell Jeremy as soon as I see him. I couldn't tell him last night. He came to visit me in Frisky's room and I think he was trying to apologize. I just..." Maren sighed, trying to find the right words. "I don't want him to be with me out of some obligation. He has serious trust issues."

"A lot of issues, yes," Tina nodded.

"It's just so embarrassing, what he did. He needs to *beg* for me in order to right things. Last night, he said, 'You look cute,' as his opening line. I can't give in to *that*. I look like an idiot for even letting him talk to me."

"Looks like he's not the only one with pride issues, at least."

Ren and Frisky wandered in. Ren sat down at a chair, saw that Frisky was chairless, and stood up, gesturing to the seat. Frisky waved her hands, as if to say, "No thank you," and the two continued to gesture at each other politely in turn.

"Oh my God, I'll take it for my feet!" Tina yanked it forward, and then stretched her legs across the upholstered seat. "Or maybe Maren should get it for her feet? That's a thing, right?" Tina smiled.

"Um, no, it's um, barely at that point." Maren laughed it off, but kept looking at Ren.

"He doesn't know?" asked Tina.

"Later," said Maren, fidgeting.

"When can we tell people?" whined Tina.

Frisky made a brave face and tucked her brown hair behind her ears. "I told him already. Sorry."

Maren frowned slightly, but then remembered Ren's loyalty. "It's okay Frisky, but I don't want anyone else to know until after I tell Jeremy."

Maren excused herself, then wandered out and found Mateo, Wantoro, and Raaychila playing a game of cards in the parlor, apparently gambling over a jar of blueberry preserves. Wantoro frowned under heavy black eyebrows. Raaychila clicked her slender fingers on her husband's arm while he determined his next move.

"Hi," mumbled Maren.

"You're doing all right, my girl?" asked Mateo. He laid his hand on the table. "Full house."

"Beats my two pair," said Raaychila. She slid the blueberry preserves across the table.

Wantoro frowned. "I thought I had it with a three-of-a-kind."

"Maren! Eat this preserve with me. Pull up a chair!" Mateo twisted the lid off. "After what you've been through," he winked, "you need to take it easy."

"Surely you'd want some bread with it," said Wantoro.

"Maren, do you want to talk about what happened?" Raaychila asked.

"Well," began Maren uncertain of how best to blurt out the news. "I, so. There's this thing—well, I wouldn't call it a thing—"

"Jeremy will come around again. His ego is just...," Raaychila nodded, unable to finish the sentence.

"Yes, yes, I know that. I..." Maren groped around awkwardly for a chair to sit on. "Please tell Jeremy to come see me if you see him around."

"Of course," said Raaychila.

Wantoro and Mateo began to shift uncomfortably. "Here, Maren," said Mateo, and he handed her the jar of blueberry preserves. Wantoro passed the bread.

CHAPTER 24

MUDDY

Mantel floated through the Maze, followed by Ms. Fritz and Jasmine. His black robe masked him completely, except a little pink flesh around his eyes, which were presently bloodshot flecks of light. "They're gone," he said. "Every last demon is gone." The torches on the stone walls led them to a stone slab covered in a thick green slime. Mantel floated over it, but Ms. Fritz had to wade through the slime. For Jasmine and her baby, however, the slime pulled back slightly, allowing Jasmine's feet to pass through unscathed. The slime coalesced quickly behind her.

When they got to the other side of the sludge, Ms. Fritz rubbed her hands together with gusto, stepping in front of Jasmine. "So then the dead will flourish? The demons won't take them from you." She smiled up at him with her thin lips, and her eyes were bright. Gorda's thick frizzy hair had been cut short, and now curly ringlets lay neatly on her forehead.

Mantel considered this. "Yes, the dead will flourish, but not for much longer. Apollyon will lead them. I don't know where he'll take them."

Ms. Fritz's cheeks turned tomato red. "Master, I know you have the answers. I never doubted you! I've seen the

Cajjez up close—I know who he is. Jeremy is no leader, he is a self-absorbed, mischievous thing. The dead belong to you and you alone will grant them the freedom that is their right! When I die, I will stay here in your Maze and I will serve you. If the dead find you, they will stay with you, not Apollyon. To hell with his demons!"

Mantel smiled wryly at Ms. Fritz, and turned to Jasmine, who was quietly nursing her baby in the shadows. "My dear flower, you've grown a fruit for me—but consider your baby spared. I do not need to consume him. Still, there's no denying the power of infants in this place. It's almost like the Maze is expecting." Mantel raised a soddy lump of flesh—what might have been an eyebrow— in Jasmine's direction. "Try setting the baby in this sludge."

"We've tried this already!" Jasmine frowned and held her baby closer. "Please, we don't have to do this. It didn't work in the other room! The Maze is not interested."

Mantel nodded to Ms. Fritz and she stepped forward and pulled the small child from Jasmine's arms. Ms. Fritz lowered the baby into the sludge. The sludge didn't budge; the baby was waist-deep in green ooze.

Jasmine cried and scooped up her dirty baby. "It didn't work."

CHAPTER 25

AN ANNOUNCEMENT

The hail had subsided and Wantoro poked his head out of the Victorian. He spotted Jeremy from a distance, took a deep breath, and jogged over to him.

Jeremy stopped short of the stairs leading up to the amphitheater and watched his father run. He wasn't used to seeing him in a frantic state. "Hello," said Jeremy, staring at his father.

"Hi," said Wantoro. He cleared his throat.

"Did you have something to tell me?" Jeremy climbed up the stairs and sat on the stage. He let his legs dangle over the side. "Dad?"

"Yes! I was in the forest the other day—it was five days ago, I think—and I learned something. That Frisko girl told me..., well Maren was with her friends. There were cannibals—"

"What!?" Jeremy scanned the distance for Maren. "I've got to find her—she didn't tell me. Is anyone hurt?"

"No, no. Forgive me, that wasn't what I wanted to talk about."

"Okay, jeez. I had no idea!" Jeremy began to chew on his fingernails.

"When a man and a woman have a strong... connection—do you know how bees pollinate the flowers?"

Jeremy shook his head. "Uh, yes? Did the cannibals breech the compound?"

"Nevermind that! The bees weren't right to talk about. I should cut straight to it."

"Okay, do."

"A man is never truly a man until he has a responsibility—do you remember when you were younger and you wanted that puppy?"

"I think? No."

"But we got you Lyrna because the puppy was needy."

"And Maren's okay?"

"Yes! You weren't ready for the puppy. But now, I think—no, you're still not ready for the puppy."

Jeremy stood up. "So everyone's okay?"

Wantoro looked back at the Victorian. "Why don't you go talk to Maren."

"I will soon. I just have to give everyone a message." Jeremy took a deep breath and stood tall. "Everyone, can I have your attention!" he yelled.

"Encore!" yelled a passerby, and some people standing beside the bulletin board started to laugh. "Take it off!"

Jeremy ignored them and took to the sky. He floated above the amphitheater and waited. There was the usual shout, followed by the buzz of the populace, all coming outside to see the spectacle. And then he heard his name.

"Jeremy!" It was Tina. "Jeremy! Get down here!"

Lyrna appeared on the stage, pawing up at Jeremy.

Jeremy ignored his pet and Tina, and instead began to glow a pale blue. The bravest drew closer to him. The more faint of heart gathered quietly along the outskirts of the town square. "I've kept this compound well supplied, but I'm going to have to ask everyone to ration your food better. You're very lucky." Jeremy wiped his brow. "There are other compounds out there, just like this. They've run out of food and water. A drought is spreading quickly from the west. Collect the hail that comes down—don't let it go to waste! I will return soon, and I'll be bringing people back here with me. You need to be hospitable." Jeremy expanded his energy and then disappeared.

Jeremy's speech threw everyone into a frenzy. Soldiers argued, tossing their hands up into the air, saying, "That was no drone! He was the one with the demons!"

Maren pushed her way through the crowd and climbed the stairs to the amphitheater. "Jeremy, come back!"

"Mew."

Maren felt a gentle paw on her knee. "Lyrna!" She picked the furry companion up by her ear tuft and then scooped up her bottom—the proper technique for fizdruft handling. "Lyrna, you have to get Jeremy for me! He's busy, I know. It sounds awful out there. I just need him to know something."

"Mew."

Maren watched the crowds disperse and then hugged Lyrna and set her down. "Tell him," Maren lifted up her shirt to reveal her belly, "I'm pregnant."

"Belly."

"Yes! My belly will get bigger." Maren lowered her shirt and pet Lyrna on the head. "Tell Jeremy about my belly.

"Big fat belly?"

"Tell him we're going to have a baby and I need to see him!"

"Meow!" Lyrna leapt into the air and disappeared into the Haze.

CHAPTER 26

FEED

It was the early morning hours in Northern Ireland and Jeremy lay on a large, cool rock thinking of the little town of Sion Mills. He could transport the lot of them back to the compound in the Hamptons. All the sheep had died and the land, he was told, had become useless. The families stuck together and seemed jovial, despite the water drying up. They'd be dead soon.

Suddenly, Lyrna popped into view. "I find! I find!" Lyrna ran around in circles.

Jeremy laughed and lay his stick down in the dirt.

"I look Boston—no. I look China—no. I find here!"

"Yes, well I had just been to Shanghai. I dropped a couple of kids off at the compound. Left them with my mom—hope she doesn't mind. More to come soon." Jeremy leaned forward and messed up Lyrna's fur.

"I like this town. I'm thinking of bringing everyone back to the compound, except for this one tall guy. I'm told he's dangerous."

"Jeremy say, 'need ration food,' I talk Maren. Maren fat!" Lyrna hopped from paw to paw.

"Oh? See, that's what I'm talking about." Jeremy rose to his feet and clenched his fist. "They have no right to be eating that much food. People are starving—but, wait... Maren? Jeremy shook his head. "Maren's not fat."

"Maren belly, soon!"

Jeremy smiled in spite of himself. "Comfort food? She misses me. But she can't eat more than the others. She wouldn't."

"Big! Fat!"

"Oh, stop Lyrna. Maren's not going to get fat," said Jeremy.

"Is."

Lyrna stretched out her paws as wide as she could. "Pregreg. Ant." Lyrna crinkled her nose at the effort.

"Huh? Pregnant?" Jeremy gasped. "Well I have to go talk to her!"

Lyrna lowered her ears. "Something coming."

Jeremy stood up and tried to march into the Haze but as he stepped through, he was blasted right out by a tremendous force and spit onto the ground. "What the hell was that?" His heart was thudding.

Something with an enormous amount of energy was traveling through the Haze, as if a planet was growing closer to the Earth. Jeremy dared to enter back into the Haze, this time bracing himself to withstand the force. He went behind the air.

A great wind was kicked up in the Haze, and while he struggled against the current, the spirit animals around him were somehow impervious. A wave of dark purple rays crashed through the Haze, which was now burning hot blue. Jeremy shielded his face from the wind with his arm, and pushed his awareness into a thick outer shield. His force field gave him a safe harbor from which he was able to look out across the Haze.

A figure approached from the darkness at the center of the force. At first, it was a green outline punctuated by intermittent flashes of a bright yellow light, but as the figure drew closer, Jeremy could see a man with dark brown skin, and his arms were lined in feathers like an eagle. The angel beat its arms again and again, and Jeremy's force field started rolling backwards with him inside, tumbling around like a mouse in a ball. He rolled right into an elephant and steadied himself against its side. The elephant lowered its head, and Jeremy was mindful of its tusks. He saw in its eyes a hierophant sitting stoically on a throne. Jeremy shook himself of the vision and braced himself, expanding his force field until it pressed into the energy of the angel.

The brown angel had no eyelids and his pupils locked with Jeremy's. The angel opened his mouth and a great wind issued forth, along with a warning: "Woe to those who dwell on the ground, and hear the angel's trumpet!"

The angel now had an eagle's beak and screeched. Jeremy covered his ears. He was blasted out of the Haze again and onto his back on the dry dirt of Sion Mills. A low rock wall crumbled and the dirt began to shift. The angel flickered in front of him and Jeremy scrambled to his feet. "Wait—"

But the angel flapped its arms, and a whirlwind knocked him back to the ground.

Jeremy sprang up, still not sure whether to fight or talk. But the angel was relentless, and it screeched and split the air. Jeremy covered his ears, and tornadoes howled around him. The eagle took to the sky, leaving Jeremy. One of the tornados tore off the roofs of the dwellings to Jeremy's left, and the debris joined the dirt and sand and swirled higher and higher. How could Jeremy fight these storms?

Jeremy attempted to weave in and out of the Haze to fly, but found that the Haze continued to push him out. *I can't fly above this. I can't fly through it.* Panic began to set in. Jeremy vibrated out a few test waves into the nearest storm. His electricity seemed to make it worse. Would he die? Could he die? He had been relying on the Haze to make him invincible, and now it was blocked to him.

The funnels swirled towards him. He clenched his energy together to anchor him in that spot as everything around him was swept into the air. Suddenly the body of a large, tall man slammed into him and was stuck there by the wind. The man was still alive and moaning, blood pouring from his mouth. Jeremy flung the man away into the wind.

Then the eagle's shadow passed overhead. "You feed the dead!" the angel said, and Jeremy could detect equal parts pity and anger in the voice. "Stop!"

Jeremy felt a darkness collect just beyond his reach. A demon had filtered through to Earth's atmosphere and was closing in on the wounded man. Jeremy concentrated on his demon. "Back," he said. But the demon pressed onward.

The man screamed at the sight of the demon and the demon pounced on him, sucking the flesh clean off his skull.

Another demon appeared beside it and another. Jeremy yelled, "Be gone!" and the demons lingered for a moment and then receded back into the Haze. "This is *not* who I am! I did not will them to eat that man! I do not feed the dead!" Jeremy looked to the sky to face the eagle angel, but he was gone.

CHAPTER 27

ZOO

Ren had been patiently instructing Tina on firearm use all morning, but Tina had a bad habit of winking at Ren right before each shot. There was a limit to the ammo one could waste on not hitting the target.

Frisky, who had observed the whole excruciating lesson, was up to bat next. "Let's try aiming at the target this time." She took the pistol from Tina and assumed the stance.

"Good, now straighten your arm and wrist out." Ren moved his hand down along Frisky's arm.

"Knock it off," Frisky snapped, and shrugged Ren off her arm. She pulled the trigger and hit the bullseye.

Ren smiled, and Tina burned with envy, resolving to focus on her strengths. "I'm going to go perfect my acrylic leopard nail design." She marched away.

"You're a natural," said Ren.

"Why would you assume that I never shot before?" Frisky replied, fidgeting with her hair. "Hey, is another hail storm moving in?" She pointed to a cluster of gray clouds swiftly approaching from the west. "We should ring the bell, get everyone ready to collect the hail."

Just then, a woman screamed from the direction that Tina had marched off to.

Frisky and Ren reflexively gripped their weapons and dashed between the dying trees and past the small barn to the perimeter fence. It was hard to believe that only a couple of days ago vegetation grew there. The dirt was dusty, and only a few weeds—now straw-like—lay in the dying Earth.

"Help!" A young boy ran up to the outside of the fence. His jeans were shredded at his knees, and there was blood and dirt caked onto his skin. He was shaking and kept looking behind him. "Please help me!"

"Who screamed?" asked Frisky.

"My sister! Please, let me in!" The boy grabbed onto the barbed wire fence and cut his hands.

"Don't!" said Ren. "Come this way."

Frisky craned her neck to see behind the boy. "What's out there?" She pulled Ren back to her. "Could be a trap," she whispered.

"Come to the main gate, you have to go through security," said Ren.

The boy rattled the fence, tears streaming down his face. "It's going to eat me!"

"It?"

"The bear! Help me, please!"

Frisky turned to Ren. "Let's just let him in."

Frisky and Ren met the boy at the north entrance of the compound. He was searched and admitted to the compound at Frisky's request. They sat him down on a bench and let the story come out.

The boy talked between sobs and coughs. "My sister, oh God, she just... and then this bear came out of nowhere and... tore her to pieces. We ran from the camp... everyone was screaming." The boy cried into his dirty sleeve.

"Let's take him to Maren," said Ren.

Maren was watching Tina pace dramatically back and forth in Maren's room.

"First of all, I'm in love with Jeremy, which everyone's known, for like, ever. But he's going to be with you, okay? And I get that. You're going to have his baby for Christ's sake. But then there's Ren and I totally called dibs on him but then Frisky's all, 'I'm going to teach you kung fu," and then they ride off into the sunset. It's not fair! Is there, like, an end-of-the-world escort service or something?"

"Tina," Maren exhaled slowly, trying to form some kind of response. "Don't." She held her hand up. "Do you feel like something big is happening?"

Tina's eyes shifted to the window. "Yeah?"

"I feel this tension, this friction." Maren stood up and opened the window. The heat from outside seeped into the window, and the room felt like a soup. "It's like a hurricane settled over our compound. Do you know about centrifugal force?"

Tina rolled her eyes. "Here comes the lecture," she grumbled.

Maren ignored her and continued. "With hurricanes, there's friction on the earth and the wind actually blows inward towards the eye of the storm. We are the eye of the storm. Something big and violent is happening outside that fence, and the storm's moving. Soon we'll no longer be in the eye—in the calm; we'll be in the Apocalypse." She held her hand up. "Do we try to outrun it? Maybe the eye will follow us, maybe not."

Tina studied her zebra print finger nails. "You don't try to outrun a storm. You go underground, like in Mantel's Maze."

Maren was quiet. She didn't know if Tina had understood anything she'd just said, but Tina's answer rang true. "I think you're right."

Ren and Frisky burst through the door with their frantic new guest. Maren and Tina looked at the boy expectantly, but he just burst into tears again.

Frisky rested her hand on the boy's shoulder. "He's from outside the compound. He told us that a flying bear attacked his sister."

Maren knitted her brows. "A flying bear? Are you sure?"

"Yes—and there were other animals too." The boy sobbed.

Maren looked at Frisky. "I sent Lyrna to find Jeremy for me. He should have been here by now."

Just then the compound's alarm system activated, and there was shouting from outside. Machine guns rattled and the rooftop artillery boomed. They ran to the window and looked in horror as the compound's defenses were routed by a swarm of animals descending from the gray sky, seemingly impervious to all weapons. It was like an entire zoo was revolting against the humans.

A rhinoceros landed on a soldier shooting at it, and crushed him into the ground. A lion roared and pounced on a fleeing woman. She held her hands up, but he mauled her and tore her apart.

Maren gasped and fell back, but Ren was there to catch her.

"I thought Jeremy said the animal spirits were good?" Ren set Maren upright.

"They were," said Maren.

CHAPTER 28

MOUNTAIN OF ASH

Wantoro finished boarding up his window. His small, clean room seemed more claustrophobic than usual.

Raaychila waited in the hallway to hear from Maren. "Any word from Jeremy?"

Maren rounded the bend and jogged towards Raaychila. "Not yet. I'm telling you, Lyrna was sane when I last saw her. Those are not Jeremy's animals."

Wantoro huffed by Maren with purpose. "I need more nails." He disappeared down the staircase.

Tina slid around the corner and rapped her acrylic nails on the wall. "If Jeremy doesn't get here soon, we have to move without him."

"But he'll know what to do about the animals," said Raaychila.

"My dad said a camp further inland is getting overrun by refugees. These animals are scattering people everywhere. We have to move soon."

"And where will we go?" asked Raaychila indignantly.

"We'll go to where Jeremy will go—to Mantel's Maze," said Tina.

The moment felt pregnant, about to burst, and then reality started to slow like a record winding down.

Everything felt heavier. They groped at the air, and then everything began to warble. Their eyes rocked back and forth as if they were in REM, and visions began to stream in. Then, as suddenly as it began, it ended, and sound and sight returned to normal, but the world was altered.

Maren lay crumpled on the floor, dreaming.

> She was floating in the sky and the sun was on her back. She cast a great shadow over the Earth. In her hands, she held an ancient book of poetry. She held it up to decipher the title and it crumbled into dust and blew away. Another book appeared in its place. It was Milraan, the religious text of the Vhasper Clan, natives of Failrun. Then it too crumbled in her hands. Another book, the Bible, appeared, and it too turned to dust when she brought it to her nose. The scene repeated over and over again, until a mountain of ash rose beneath her and met her feet. She sank into the dust, stretching her arms up overhead.

"What the hell was that?" said Tina. She helped Maren to her feet and brushed Maren's long blonde hair from her face. "Hey!" Tina slapped at Maren's cheeks.

"Am I...?" Maren wiped her forehead. She had scraped it on the edge of a desk when she fell. Blood was on her hand. She wiped it on her black yoga pants.

Just then, something bashed against the boarded window, splintering the wood. And again. The boards and glass parted, and a raccoon with wild eyes burst through, screeching and clawing at the air. Wantoro grabbed a lamp and smashed it on the raccoon, but the raccoon simply fluffed up and hissed, unaffected by the blow. Everyone backed up, and the critter scurried down the hallway.

"Follow me!" Tina ran in the direction of the raccoon "We'll load everyone into the tanks!"

General Forero and Anna—Tina's mother—met with Tina, Maren, Frisky, Ren, Wantoro, Raaychila, and Mateo outside. A flock of spirit animals were circling overhead. A couple of dead shrubs had caught on fire and smoke began to fill the air, adding to the chaos. As a man was running back towards the Victorian home, a swarm of spirit animals dove downwards in formation, led by a horse. They descended on him in a frenzy like piranhas.

Tina took advantage of the distraction and ran to the front gate of the perimeter fence to a large gray tank. "Get in!" Tina jumped into the hatch just as a huge gust of wind sent debris flying across the yard.

"Where are you going?" shouted General Forero. He chased after her, and dodged a torn sign post that whipped past his head.

"I know of somewhere safe! Somewhere the animals can't go!" She didn't know if that was true, but she knew that that was the only other place where they might reunite with Jeremy.

A spirit animal dove towards Frisky, and Maren yanked her forward. The spirit animal turned and swooped towards an old woman, who was fleeing in the opposite direction. Maren and Frisky ran a few more feet, than climbed in the tank next, followed by Ren.

"We'll get in this one!" shouted Wantoro, and he threw open the hatch of the second tank.

"Wait, you're going too?" General Forero turned and looked at his fortress, now in ruin. The left wall of his beautiful Victorian was on fire and spirit animals were dragging bodies out by the dozen.

"Yes!" said Wantoro, as he helped Raaychila into the tank. "Get as many as you can to follow us. Or they can stay here and die."

Each tank could fit roughly five to six people. The tanks had been stripped of everything non-essential. Even the original plush seating had been ripped up and replaced with wooden planks. General Forero had been worried about defending a base, not escaping one. "This is suicide," said Frisky as the tank rolled forward. She gripped the metal in front of her for support.

"Ren, you've driven this thing, help me navigate!" Tina turned around from the cockpit. "And Frisky, if you're going to continue to be all doom and gloom, you can walk if you want to."

"Watch the road!" yelled Ren. The tank hit a tall, withered tree; it teetered.

"Reverse!" cried Maren. But another tank was tailgating them. The dead tree fell and crumbled under the treads. Then there was a clap like thunder.

"What was that?" said Frisky.

All the trees around them began to teeter and crash. The tank rolled onward, bulldozing through the debris. Then beetles emerged from the rotten cores of the trees and covered the outside of the tanks. The walls of the tank vibrated under the beating of a million wings, until at last the beetles took to the sky in search of some new carcass host.

CHAPTER 29

WE'RE HERE

The tank rumbled to a stop in front of what was left of the Donegall Estate. The privacy fence was long gone. The grass was replaced with blotches of dried yellow weeds and dirt. The streets were empty and spirit animals soared ominously in the darkening sky.

"We're here," said Tina. "How many tanks do we have?"

Ren lifted the hatch and popped his head out. "I'm counting seven, no eight. One's coming around the corner." Another tank rolled into sight, its wheels crushing sheets of metal and rotten plywood.

"Close it!" Frisky grabbed Ren's legs and pulled him down. The hatch locked back into place.

The other tanks pulled up onto the Donegall property, and were positioned around the hot spring—a small pool of water surrounded by a neat stone formation. A plume of water vapor billowed up from the ground.

"So now what?" asked Frisky. "We're all that's left?"

"We'll wait for Jeremy," said Maren. "Maybe the others will find... other ways to escape?"

Frisky sighed. "We're safe in here. I bet people are hiding out in the jets." She leaned forward and tapped at a peephole. "I don't think the animals can get in here."

146

The sky lit up and a lightning bolt splintered a dead, gnarled tree just left of the tank. It fell on its side with a great thud and caught fire. More thunder.

Maren closed her eyes and exhaled.

And then there was a knock on the hatch.

"Let him in!" shouted Tina, and Ren jumped up and threw open the hatch. "Jeremy!"

Frisky smiled despite herself.

Maren looked down at her lap.

Jeremy hopped into the tank and scooched beside Maren. "Hey," he said. "Hey!" He reached for her belly and pressed his hand against it. "Look at me."

Maren covered her hands over her face.

"What's going on with the animals, Jeremy?" blurted Frisky.

Jeremy paused, annoyed that his moment was interrupted by business. "The border between the Haze and Earth's atmosphere collapsed. I can't hide in the Haze anymore, and the spirit animals are in some kind of frenzy. And there was this eagle, and this wind. I just wanted to see Maren." Jeremy turned to her, leaned in, and tried to gently pry her hands from her face. "Talk to me, Maren."

Tina smacked the back of Jeremy's head, "So just to clarify, you know that your cute spirit pets are eating people, right?"

Jeremy winced. "What?"

Maren withdrew her hands from her wet face, but still wouldn't look at Jeremy. "We should go into Mantel's Maze."

CHAPTER 30

GET DOWN

Jeremy scrambled up through the hatch. The last of the clouds dispersed overhead and starlight pierced the hazy sky, which had taken on a soft purple hue. The spirit animals were far above the tanks, flying like shooting stars across the sky. "Maren, you *will* talk to me. Just let me see the animals. I don't think they've spotted us here yet. Oh, hey! There's my dad."

Frisky shook her head, exasperated, as Jeremy's shoe kicked her in the cheek on his way up. Frisky snapped the hatch shut behind him. "He's not taking this seriously."

Maren opened the hatch again and poked her head out. "Get us into Mantel's Maze and then find Lyrna. I don't feel safe with these animals around." Maren pointed to the hot spring and it sprayed steam in response. "Jeremy, it's active. We should go down now."

"You really want to go down there again?" Jeremy frowned at the bubbling pool. "Hold on a second. Let me see if it's working." Jeremy jumped into the hot spring and the membrane parted for him. He floated down the familiar shoot and after the thick clouds of water vapor cleared, he could see the sides of the tunnel lit up by otherworldly torches. He drifted for a time, stretching out his awareness, and when he felt reasonably assured, he glided back up and landed on the scorched grass. "Well, I don't sense any spirit animals down there," said Jeremy. "Maybe they can't go in for some reason. I don't know if it's going to be any better."

Wantoro climbed out of his tank. "I'll go down first with Raaychila. Just guide us down nice and steady, if you will, and we'll wait at the bottom."

Jeremy nodded at his father, proud to be of brave stock.

"Folks," Jeremy rose slightly in the air and emanated a blue aura. "Everyone lift up your hatch and listen!" he yelled. "Now, you've seen what I'm capable of at this point. I can fly," he took to the sky and then landed gently on the ground, "I can zap," he shot a lightning bolt behind him, "and I look good doing it."

Tina snickered.

"So here's the plan," he used his diaphragm to project the words. "We're all going to jump into that hot spring," he pointed. "We'll do this in an orderly fashion. The descent is safe—you'll float down. Trust me. My parents are going in first."

He had to dislodge some of the surrounding stones to make room for his mother's wheelchair. The portal to the Maze widened for her, and Jeremy helped his parents down the passageway. The chute opened up to the underground Maze—the graveyard chamber. Jeremy set his parents down and scanned the rows of headstones.

Meanwhile, on the surface, everyone sat in their tanks and waited. The seconds ticked by.

Maren pressed her eye to a slit and peered out. The air outside looked still. "Think we should line people up?"

"Let's wait for Jeremy," said Frisky. "I'd just... feel more comfortable."

"It's really easy to go down, it just takes a leap of faith," said Maren.

"Better than getting sucked into an ocean vortex, I hope?" Tina laughed, but when she met Frisky's eyes, added, "that's how I got to Mantel's Maze. I'm sure going through boiling water is much better."

Maren took a deep breath and then opened the tank's hatch. "As soon as Jeremy comes up from the hot spring, we'll begin emptying the tanks," she called out. "Our tank will go first, and we'll work clockwise."

The hatch on the tank opposite the hot spring opened up and the head of a man popped out. "We've been talking in here and we think we should just stay in the tanks. We'll have runners forage for food and water. The tanks are safe. Makes no sense to go underground."

"What about the earthquakes?" A woman's head poked out of the next tank over. "We'll be buried alive! I'm sorry, but I'm not going to put my faith in 'Chippendale.'"

"Everyone, get down!" Mateo was looking out from the tank beside Maren's, and he pointed behind her. "A swarm's coming!" In the distance, a cloud of spirit animals approached like a nest of angry wasps, flying close to the ground. In the wake of the swarm, dirt and dust swirled like tornadoes. Everyone closed their hatches and bunkered down.

They watched the video monitors in silence as the animals grew larger and descended on them. An elephant thudded down next to one of the tanks, stood on its hind legs, and began to rock the tank back and forth with its front legs.

"Search for weapons, anything," said Ren.

Maren spoke with her hand over her mouth. "We should have gone in when we had the chance."

They heard a loud hiss outside the tank.

"That better not be what it sounds like!" said Tina.

An adder slithered through one of the small holes in the tank, and they all leapt back. It struck at the air a few times, but got caught in the hole at its fat middle. Frisky handed Ren a large Bowie knife which he unsheathed. He waited for the snake to strike the air again, and then he countered with a chop to the snake's head while it was recoiling. The knife just glanced off.

At the same time in the tank next door, General Forero and Anna were arming themselves. General Forero took the shotgun, and Anna took a small pistol. A guy who they barely knew named Ralph began to rock back and forth in his seat, saying "no, no." Mateo nervously twiddled his thumbs next to him.

"How are you going to shoot that thing from in here?" asked Anna, gesturing to the General's shotgun.

The General frowned. "Good point. I should have the pistol."

"I think you both make good points," offered Mateo.

"Why should you have it?" snapped Anna.

There was a metal scraping noise and a crash and they could see on the monitor that three elephants had overturned one of the tanks.

The General grabbed the gun from Anna and aimed through one of the slits in the tank, and shot a bull that was charging another tank straight in the eye. The bullet glanced off, and Anna stuck her fingers in her ears. The bull turned and charged their tank instead. Just then there was screeching above the tank, and several massive eagles opened the hatch above them.

Jeremy burst out of the hot spring, and his heart skipped a beat. "Stop!" The spirit animals ignored him.

To Jeremy's horror, an eagle dove into a tank and pulled out poor Ralph, who was screaming "no, no!" and the animals swarmed him. A tiger shark and a gorilla joined in on the feast, and Ralph was torn limb from limb.

Jeremy flashed over to Maren's tank, and pulled the snake out of the hole and tossed it aside. "You have to get in the hot spring! I have an idea." Jeremy raised his arms. "Demons," he said, and his demons appeared in droves, menacing the spirit animals. An elephant sounded its trunk and a goat bleated. The spirit animals retreated while the demons spread out, and the hatch of one tank popped open and people began to evacuate.

"Go," shouted the woman on top of the tank, and the

people fled towards an abandoned building across the street. In their haste, they ignored Jeremy's frantic motioning towards the hot spring. A nearby wolf leapt on the woman leading the pack. Jeremy flashed over to the woman, but then saw an eagle rise out of his parents' tank with Mateo in its talons. The great bird hovered and flapped for a moment with its weighty captive, and then the eagle was pierced by the horns of a demon, causing it to drop Mateo. Jeremy rushed in and caught him before he hit the ground, and then tossed him like a sack of potatoes into the hot spring.

The wolf was tearing the woman into shreds, and she let out a blood-curdling scream.

"Everyone jump in!" Jeremy yelled, and he shot over to Maren, Tina, and Frisky, and then dumped them into the hot spring. A baboon threw a demon off of its back, sending it soaring through a man trying to get to the hot spring. The man fell on his knees and began to convulse. A pack of rats descended on him, and Jeremy dashed over and began picking them off like leaches. *This isn't working.*

Jeremy stood up, and pushed his energy out in a dome, and where he felt a spirit animal, he made the energy hard, and where he felt a person, he made it soft. The demons were unaffected. He pushed the energy out like an expanding screen, and was able to sift the animals from the people. Everyone got to their feet and scrambled towards the bubbling pool in a blind terror. Some thirty-odd people jumped into the hot spring while Jeremy pushed back the animals. He called more demons forth, and the spirit animals took to the sky. "Be gone!" he shouted, and he watched them fly into the distance. Then Jeremy found abandoned personal effects—a purse, a shoe, a knife, a water bottle—and dropped them into the hot spring. Empty tanks, ruins, and corpses were strewn around. *This is all my fault.* Jeremy posted sentry demons around the entrance to Mantel's Maze, willing them to hold their position until he called on them. Maybe the demons would prevent the spirit animals from entering. He jumped into the hot spring.

CHAPTER 31

BUDDING HOPE

Jeremy drifted to the bottom and approached the rest of the party. Everyone was hushed, looking down dark caverns and row after row of tombstones. A few feet from the hot spring's drop-off point, Maren was standing alone in a corner. A gentle breeze blew through the room, and little lights began to glow around Maren. Tiny green plant buds were sprouting up from the stone around her, emitting a soft light.

Jeremy stepped through the crowd, some thirty-odd refugees, and made his way to Maren. He bit his lip. "We made it."

"We did."

"I can be such a jerk, right?" Jeremy leaned forward and kissed Maren on the cheek.

Maren nodded.

He pressed his finger on her lips, then pushed it into her mouth.

Maren closed her eyes for a second, and then swatted his hand away. "You're even a jerk when you're trying to apologize."

"Sorry." He held his hands up. "Sensuality is gentle. I am trying, here."

"What are you sorry for?" Maren crossed her arms.

Jeremy sighed. "Oh God, Maren, everything. I'm sorry I doubted your ridiculously stupid glow-in-the-dark watch stunt. I'm sorry I have impulse-control problems. I'm sorry I'm a pervert. I'm sorry that I'm so bad at saying sorry."

Jeremy knelt down before her, lifted her shirt up, and kissed her belly. "But I'm not sorry for this. I love you."

Maren ran her fingers through his hair. "Okay."

Jeremy stood up and wrapped his arms around her. Then he kissed her.

Maren drew the kiss out, savoring the moment. He tasted so good and she felt warm all over.

At last, Jeremy pulled back. "We lost a lot of people. Where do we go now?"

Maren reached down and touched one of the buds and it bloomed into a small yellow flower. "We need to go to an oasis."

"The one by Fedonis? So what, we take the submarine? With this group?" Jeremy frowned. "I suppose they'll need a briefing."

A thin vine pushed out from the stone and began to snake around Maren's foot. "Oh!" She pulled it free with ease. "Do you see this?" The stone began to rumble softly and a colony of vines twirled its way out of the stone, creating a thick matted path into one of the chambers. It turned a corner.

"We should follow it," said Maren.

"No!" Tina pushed her way into their huddle. "Someone get TP, because you've got to be shitting me. It's just a stupid trick like always."

Jeremy winced. "Gross, Tina."

"We should just check," said Maren.

Horror spread across Jeremy's features. "Wait! Mantel will try to get our baby. Maren, do not follow those vines! In fact," Jeremy marched towards the hot spring passageway, "we need to get out of here. Terrible idea, I've decided."

"Wait!" Maren stepped towards him. "We have to follow the vines, Jeremy."

"Don't you remember, Maren?" Jeremy slid onto the stone floor and leaned up against a headstone. He put his head in his hands. "Mantel believes he'll grow stronger if he can eat babies. This is all orchestrated."

The pack of refugees was eavesdropping on the whole conversation, and began to murmur at the prospect of baby-eating. "Hey, we can't live in a graveyard!" yelled a man. "I refuse to stay here," yelled a frantic woman. "Who's in charge around here?" yelled another.

"I am," said Maren, turning to face them.

Jeremy sat upright, but held his tongue. The General also flinched.

Tina stepped forward. "Maren's in charge, okay? She knows this place."

"I vote for Vor Wantoro," said a man, pointing to Wantoro. He saluted him.

Wantoro smiled. "What we need is someone with fresh, clear eyes and a strong heart. Someone who always sees the path in the dark. Maren Nononia's been here before and has wandered these dusty corridors with my son. Jeremy is powerful, but Maren is a beacon. She will guide us along to safety."

Then Tina remembered back to the time she was a Mantel's Maze newbie, and put her hands on her hips. "And just so everyone knows, it's about to get really trippy down here. Ghosts, talking ferrets, rainbow rocks, and even weird gross old men with theme songs. So you might as well start freaking out now and get it over with before we move."

The crowd began to bicker.

"But," said Maren, holding up her hand, "there's also an oasis and it will provide all the sustenance you'll ever need. It's refreshing too, like a citrus fruit."

"All right," said Jeremy, standing up. He dusted his butt off. He leaned over to Maren and whispered in her ear. "We can follow the vines for a little bit, but the first whiff of danger and I'm going to fly you straight out of this place."

Maren walked forward and beckoned for everyone to follow her and they did. The trail of vines and buds led her deep into the heart of the catacombs. Torches jutted out from the ceiling at odd angles. The room itself was too expansive to see from one side to the other. Occasionally, the ceiling would connect to the ground in a snaky pillar of rock. Dusty tombstones were jutting out of the ground. Maren brushed one off and read its inscription:

> Here Lies the Remains of Gestapo Valencia,
> With a hint of amaretto and a cherry finish,
> In his stead, a leather upholstered foot-rest
> Massages Master's feet.

Maren turned to Jeremy, who was at her side. "I can hear voices from the vines. See how they grow out of the graves? Inside the graves are scraps of souls that Mantel didn't eat. These souls are resentful. They came here to Mantel on the promise of everlasting life without being sorted, only to become one of Mantel's foot rests.... How would you feel?"

"Like a rebellious servant."

"The vines are growing out of the soul pieces. They want to help us."

Jeremy listened a moment, but heard no voices. "If you say so, Maren."

They continued to walk past the tombstones and rounded the corner of a particularly large stone formation until the path led to a wall of vines, and they hit a dead end. Maren knelt down and touched the ground. The vines began to squirm under her hands, and parted, and dirt crumbled into a small hole in the ground. Below, they could see a tangle of roots beneath the catacombs.

"Maren," Jeremy began to widen the hole with his hands. "We won't be able to get all these people down there. I don't even know if I can fit down there, and I'm the fittest person in this whole group."

Maren leaned forward. "I'll go first, but... how far to the bottom is it?"

"Yeah, let's just send the pregnant girl into the dangerous hole. How far along are you anyway?" Jeremy rubbed her belly, sighed, and then eased his way into the hole, hanging onto a stone with one hand. The vines began to slither slowly beneath him, hollowing out a tunnel going down. He emitted a soft, blue light, and looked into the tunnel, but he couldn't see the bottom. He then grabbed two fistfuls of vines, and began to climb down.

"So far so good," he called out, only a deep chill washed over him. About forty grueling feet down in that claustrophobic tunnel, he reached a bottom of sorts. The dirt was a rich loam, with a deep earth smell. The vines were slowly receding away from him, hollowing out a clearing in the slithering jungle. He dimmed his blue light and allowed his eyes to adjust. Thin beams of torchlight from the catacombs above began to pierce the jungle, as the vines shifted. It seemed on purpose.

"Still good," he called up.

Somehow they all managed to get down there, even Raaychila with the manly assistance of Wantoro. The party clung together and awaited direction.

"What now, Maren?" asked Jeremy.

"Keep your light going, please. Do you hear that water?"

Jeremy lifted his palm up and emanated more soft blue light, which intermingled with shadows. All around them were structures of vine and dirt, and vines criss-crossing from the ceiling to the ground. Maren walked into the jungle followed by Jeremy, and the roots and vines parted into a path. They walked in silence, twisting and turning through some hundred yards, before arriving in front of a stone wall. Multi-colored blossoms began to pop out of the cracks in the stone, traveling up the wall until they formed a cluster forty feet up.

"Break a hole in that ceiling, Jeremy."

"I thought you'd never ask."

Jeremy struck a dramatic pose and angled his palms upward. He blasted the wall a few times where the blossoms had clustered. The stone crumbled with ease and Jeremy could see the torchlight streaming through from above. "This place needed some lighting." Almost on command, the vines formed a ladder and Jeremy climbed up, taking his time to inspect the latticework. At the top, he reached through the hole and could feel a hollow inside with a smooth wall. "It's a room," he called down.

"Jeremy, a little light?"

"Oh, right." Jeremy sent a beam back into the root network.

"Nevermind, we have Ren's watch." Maren climbed up after him and Jeremy rolled his eyes. They wriggled through the opening.

Jeremy called behind him. "Good news up here!"

A large green pool bubbled in the center of the stone room, sending out a mellow steam. Torches stuck out of each of the four corners shining multi-colored light: one red, one blue, one yellow, and one green. There was a wooden door at the opposite end and it was dark brown and polished.

Jeremy leaned over the edge of the deep green pool, cupped his hands and drank the cool liquid. "Tastes good. Do you think it's okay for the baby?"

Maren leaned over the water's edge and drank from the oasis. "I'm so thirsty. The baby's more at risk from dehydration than dark magic."

"An oasis, did I hear right?" Mateo popped his head out of the hole, panting from the climb. "Hey!" He called behind him. "Come up and have a drink, everyone!" There was laughter and cheers as everyone soon piled into the room to drink from the oasis and replenish their spirits.

CHAPTER 32

LOCK ARMS

Maren decided they would set up camp in the root network, as she trusted the souls of the roots. The enemy of her enemy was her friend. The jungle was receptive to its new guests, and the roots thinned out in a center area to form a sort of campsite surrounded by small cave-like structures hollowed out in the mounds of dirt and vines. Jeremy carefully removed sod and rock from the cracks in the tangled ceiling of the root network, and a thin torch light flickered down, illuminating their campsite in a dappled, golden light.

But some refugees were still ill at ease. "I still think Vor Wantoro should be in charge—he was a king in the Farmoore Galaxy and he can keep his son in check."

"Jeremy's nothing but a playboy," another agreed. Maren was again overlooked.

One of General Forero's men piped up, "It was the General who rallied us on the surface. He protected us and built a new home. Why shouldn't he continue to lead us?"

"Vor Wantoro could beat General Forero in any way, shape, or form."

Now the party broke into two halves, and Jeremy and Maren—who were at the other end of the campsite admiring the root network—took notice and returned to them.

"What's going on?" asked Jeremy. "Have we not found you drink and shelter?" He crossed his arms, and then looked at his father whose eyebrows were raised and strained—a look Jeremy was familiar with. "What's wrong?" asked Jeremy.

"I'll tell you what's wrong," said General Forero, stepping forward. "I'm challenging Vor Wantoro to an arm wrestling match."

The crowd cheered.

Jeremy leaned in to Maren and whispered, "Have they gone mad?"

Maren shrugged.

Vor Wantoro stepped forward. "I accept."

Jeremy's jaw dropped. He looked at his father's meaty forearms, nodded, then looked to General Forero's slightly meatier forearms. "Are you sure this is a good idea, Dad?"

Wantoro laughed. "It's okay, just a bit of fun. We need to get our mind off of things." Then he made his game face, his thick black brows set in a fierce V, his square jaw locked, and his blue eyes narrowed on his opponent.

Jeremy sighed and Tina pushed him aside.

"Go, daddy! You can do it!" She hopped from foot to foot and clapped her hands. Meanwhile, a group of men had started to roll a massive rock they'd found to a room-sized cove. They set it down and then formed chairs out of clumps of strong, thick vines. Vor Wantoro and General Forero ducked below some hanging vines and took a seat across from each other, then extended their arms and locked hands. So it began.

The two men flared their nostrils and set their mouths in tight lines. They kept their arms close to their bodies for leverage. Wantoro did a test push and the General bit his bottom lip a little, but the arm didn't move. The veins in their forearms bulged magnificently, and Jeremy was in awe of the vascular manliness. Wantoro did another test push, and the General counterattacked by pulling Wantoro's arm towards him. The General's bicep contracted fiercely.

"Hssssssssss!" said Wantoro.

A man in the crowd began to describe the match like a sports announcer.

Wantoro leaned forward, rolled his hand around the General's, and pried it open a small amount, gaining one of the small advantages that could eventually accumulate into a victory. All of the veins in the General's face bulged.

The match continued in this manner for about fifteen minutes. The crowd grew less excited by the spectacle as the minutes went on.

"All right," said a woman in the crowd, "I guess I should ... go check on the vines."

"Yeah, me too," said someone else.

"Woooooooohhhhh! Team Forero!" hollered Tina.

A man in the crowd yawned and pretended to check a watch. The sports fans offered various excuses and began to filter out, one by one, until Jeremy, Maren, and Tina were the sole observers of the epic duel.

"Enough!" said Jeremy, and broke their hands apart.

"This is a waste of time."

Wantoro and the General's right arms fell to their sides. They tried to put them on the rock again, but could not. Each was covered in sweat and heaving, now having a staring match.

"You sonofabitch," said General Forero, and both men snapped their left arms onto the rock, and the battle continued. Jeremy was exasperated and threw up his hands. He walked out of the room, followed sheepishly by Maren. Tina opened her mouth to cheer her daddy on, but then closed it. A minute later, she left. Hours passed.

Vor Wantoro and General Forero were weak and clammy. Their arms pathetically trembled, each exerting the force of a single ant.

"Oo-oo-aaah."

"All the way to the end, you wimp!" yelled General Forero.

"I've got this," said Wantoro.

"Oo-oo-aaah-aaah!" It was a shrill call, and it was close by.

Vor Wantoro and General Forero both cocked their heads to the side and saw it: an orange monkey with big round eyes and flared nostrils. It hissed and bared its fangs. The men leapt up and held their weak arms out to prevent the attack, but the monkey charged.

General Forero attempted the first slap. It was in slow motion and more like a petting motion than anything else. The monkey beat its chest and bit the air in a fierce display.

Wantoro stroked its cheek with half a fist.

"Help!" General Forero and Vor Wantoro backed away, then took turns kicking their large, inflexible legs at the beast. It mounted the table and then beat its chest again.

Jeremy, Maren, and Tina ran forward, but as soon as Jeremy saw the monkey, he shooed everyone back. "It could be a spirit animal! Dad, General Forero, run!" Jeremy lunged at the monkey and it hissed and sprang off the table towards a low-hanging vine. Jeremy, the faster of the two, caught up to it and grabbed its tail. The monkey screamed and grabbed hold of Jeremy's hair, yanking with all its might. Jeremy knocked it back with his hand. "Not a spirit animal!" he shouted back to his friends and family. Jeremy sent a blue bolt past the creature, and the monkey skittered up the vine and disappeared. "Good riddance!"

Jeremy walked back over to the crowd of onlookers. "Just a regular old amalgamation of souls molded into a monkey. Don't be too alarmed, folks."

Mateo shot a hand-gun at Jeremy. "Guess we shouldn't monkey around down here."

Maren groaned.

* * *

Once everyone had settled into various nooks and crannies, Jeremy pulled Maren aside. "How you feeling?"

"Fine," she said, sizing him up. "Why?"

"Come with me on the surface?"

Maren nodded.

Jeremy and Maren wriggled up out of the root network and back into the mass graveyard. It was just as gray and dusty as they'd left it. Jeremy stretched and did some jumping jacks.

"Should I take this as a warning?" She stretched too.

"I want to show you how fast I can go. I've got finesse."

"Are you sure you don't want to practice a few times without me?" Maren was unsure whether she trusted him to carry her and work out his angel-skills simultaneously.

He scooped her up regardless and slung her over his shoulder, giving her butt an obnoxious slap, and he raced towards the hot spring entrance, accelerating as he went. He made a long jump over all the gravestones that jutted up, covering the length of the graveyard in mere seconds, and landed like a cat softly on the other side. The collapse of the Haze had its perks. Maren was a little tensed up, the wind blowing all of her hair straight out from her face.

They reached the spot where the tunnel to the Donegall Estate led up from the ceiling. Jeremy squatted low with Maren in his arms, and then shot up into the tunnel with its carnival lights. They burst through the membrane of the hot spring at the Donegall Estate and into the atmosphere, a dull morning glow all around them, and then landed on the scorched ground like ballet dancers. Jeremy put Maren on her feet and held her up under her armpits. "Not too dizzy?"

Maren stabilized and then brushed her hair off of her face. "What if the speed was too much for the baby?" Maren crossed her arms and glowered at Jeremy.

Jeremy's eyes roamed the sky. "That baby's at least half angel, he probably loved it." Jeremy winked at Maren, knowing he was pressing a button with the pronoun.

Suddenly to their left, shrieks came out of a dilapidated apartment complex. Jeremy considered investigating, but then there was a long silence. He was too late.

Maren grimaced and began to fan her face. "Hey—it's getting hotter out here."

Jeremy looked at the sky. "Lyrna!" he called out. The world felt empty, and the sky began to blacken. A dark cloud in the distance rolled towards them, and red lights began flashing in the smoke. A shadow spread across the ruined landscape. Then—darkness.

"The Apocalypse got style," Jeremy said.

A crest of light gathered on the horizon.

"It's the sun!" said Maren, pointing.

The sun slipped higher and higher into the sky, but soon passed overhead and gave way to darkness once more.

"How is that even possible? Let's go back to the Maze," said Maren with her hand on her stomach.

CHAPTER 33

MOSSING AND MEOWING

"Maren, I can't sleep." Tina crawled through the entrance to Maren and Jeremy's den, which was carpeted in moss. The roots intertwined elegantly above them in a spacious dome. Jeremy and Maren were spooning on a large moss couch, Maren facing out with her eyes closed. Jeremy raised his head from behind her and gave Tina the stink eye.

"Ménage à troi?" suggested Tina as she crawled on her hands and knees towards them.

"Tina, get out." Jeremy turned onto his stomach and tucked his head into his arm. Maren's eyes fluttered open.

"Nice moss. Comfy digs. Hey!" Tina crawled over to the moss couch and rubbed Maren's belly a little. "You guys have the penthouse!"

"What?" Maren rubbed her eyes. "We're trying to sleep, Tina."

"Right, sleep." Tina made air quotes.

An awkward silence ensued.

"All right guys, make sure you stay on your schedule. Just thought we might have an end of the world party." Tina rolled her eyes, and crawled back out of the room.

Jeremy and Maren exchanged grumbles, and soon fell into an uneasy sleep.

The next morning, Jeremy and Maren emerged from their den to find Tina, Frisky, and Ren sitting on an extra thick root. Torch light flickered down through the small cracks in the root ceiling, illuminating everyone's faces in a soft, golden light. Jeremy and Maren joined them on the root.

"Is it just me, or is time... off?" said Ren. "My watch still had some juice in it, but it's going crazy."

Maren massaged her temples. "The cycle of the earth is all sped up. The sun and moon just pass overheard like this." Maren made an arc with her hand. "We went to the surface last night."

Everyone quieted and took in the incomprehensible news.

"I guess that explains the beard." Frisky rubbed Ren's uncharacteristically furry chin.

"And Maren's belly. Maren, your butt is mossing!" said Tina, pointing. They all stood up from the root except Maren, and watched as moss was spreading around her butt.

Tina jumped up and down and giggled wildly. "Come to my little hut! You *have* to! I can't sleep on the dirt anymore." Tina began to squeal, as though this detail of the conversation was the most pertinent.

"Oh, well okay." Maren tried to twist around to look at her own butt.

Tina grabbed Maren's hand and led her forward.

Maren made her rounds to the caves of the refugees, furnishing each with structures of vines and moss. Tiny flowers blossomed as she worked the plants into useful clumps. She felt like a snake charmer, coaxing the plants to slither here and there.

Maren built walls to enclose the caves, and the refugees appreciated the privacy. She formed benches in the main cavern to create a meeting place. Finally, Jeremy brought her up to the ceiling of the cavern, and she formed torch holders, which Jeremy stocked with pilfered torches from the catacombs, brightening everyone's mood.

Maren and Jeremy sat on a vine bench for a time in silence. People milled about, finding ways to hoard oasis juice in their caves.

"The Dodgkin boys are trying to get me to make some of the rooms near the oasis into meadows. I think I will."

Jeremy smiled and walked with her back to their improved dwelling on the outskirts of the main cavern. "You've given people hope, and you've made something dismal into something lovely." He kissed her hand. "But don't wander too far. You and I both know the Maze isn't all flowers and warm feelings."

"Yeah," she said, laying down on the moss. "Right. Going to try to find Lyrna again?"

"Yup."

The surface world had grown hotter still, and the air smelled like smoke and burnt matter. Wild fires were everywhere, and every building was in rubble or close to it. The sun over the Donegall Estate had all but bleached out the colors of the world. The trees, the hedges surrounding the property were no more, and a sickness collected in the pit of Jeremy's stomach as he considered his own castle and everything that once was in the Farmoore Galaxy. Then Lyrna appeared beside him and interrupted his reverie. She wove herself around his legs in a figure eight pattern and purred loudly.

"Lyrna!" Jeremy scratched behind her ear. "It's about time!" He kissed her fluffy cheek.

"Mew!" she began to purr.

He scooped her up.

"We're down here." He made for the hot spring. Lyrna pushed against his chest with her paws, sticking her claws through his shirt. "No," she said.

"We're all down there. Maren's down there."

"Talk here."

"Why are the spirit animals attacking people?" The sun and moon flew by again, then again. Jeremy winced as the claws pushed in deeper. "Ow! Hey—will you attack our friends if you go into the Maze?"

Lyrna meowed sadly.

"Okay, tell me everything you know."

Lyrna nodded and unravelled some truth.

CHAPTER 34

A HARD TRUTH

Jeremy closed his eyes and meditated. Now he was above himself, looking down. One breath lasted a long time. He looked at the tangled root wall. He was looking at himself. Time doesn't matter; *But it's time*, a little voice said to him in the back of his mind. Jeremy breathed in and slowly came to.

Jeremy had taken a short pit stop to an uninhabited corner of the root jungle. No torch light touched this corner. His mind swarmed with all possible directions and their consequences. What he'd learned from Lyrna—he couldn't bring himself to tell Maren—not yet.

CHAPTER 35

SHADOW

Jeremy and Maren slept on their bed of moss, their limbs entangled. There was a commotion outside their hut. Maren shook Jeremy awake.

"Yeah? Oh." He heard the noise.

Together, they parted the vine fringe that was their door and walked outside. A dozen or so people were gathered in the meeting area, talking in low voices.

Mateo was sitting on a bench, and jolted up and shuffled over to Maren.

"What's up?" she asked.

"Some of the kids just came in from the meadows. Said they heard a strange sound. Ren went to investigate. I told him to wait, but these people don't understand the dangers of this place."

Maren drummed her fingers on her arm. "He shouldn't have gone out, you're right."

"Oh, Ms. Maren!" A young boy of seven years ran to her and flapped his arms excitedly. "A noise like a growl, like a big hiss, but a shadow too!"

"You did not see a shadow!" said the other boy, yanking the other's sleeve.

"I did!"

"Well then how come I didn't see it?"

"Because you were running and I looked back."

"Okay," said Maren. "And where was the shadow?"

"It was by the door, on the wall, but there wasn't anything to give it a shadow!"

The crowd started to panic a little. Wantoro knew what to do.

"Everyone just calm down," he boomed. "You've seen what my son can do, he will protect us. Look, just like in the forest on the surface, there are some wild animals down here. But as long as we stay together, they won't even bother us. Nobody should be out wandering alone, especially children. And we should post a continuous watch. I'll take the first shift. Everyone just go back in your shelters, and go back to sleep. When everyone wakes up, we should all talk about more organization around here." Wantoro crossed his arms, and people began to walk back to their huts. But then a howl came out of the root jungle, and ended in a growl. The torches went out.

In the sudden blackness, the children began to scream. Maren gasped and felt around her for Jeremy. "Jeremy?" she called out. Her feet found the entryway back into her cave and she waited there for a second. "Jeremy!" *He's gone out to find the beast.*

Maren wandered down the root hall towards the ladder to the oasis room. She reached the vine lattice and scaled it quickly. The pool was just in front of her.

Another howl echoed around the root jungle.

She heard Mateo and Wantoro shouting for her at the bottom. She continued to run through the darkness, around the oasis. She reached the door on the other side, groped around for the handle, and flung it open. There was the meadow she just grew, and she could feel the new moss under her toes in the darkness. The beast howled again from behind the door on the other end of the meadow room. Then the door swung open and a blue light blinded her.

"Maren!" It was Jeremy. "What are you doing? Are you insane?" He closed the door behind him, but something caught it.

"Behind you!" she cried.

A massive brown paw had stopped the door, and Jeremy brought his light down. The paw was clawing at the moss at the base of the door.

"Don't hurt it!" yelled Maren.

Jeremy electrified his body and formed thick blue plates of armor around himself. "Demon," he said in a flat voice, and a demon shimmered next to him, darkness bending around it.

"Jeremy! I have to give it something."

The beast nudged the door open and poked a snout into the meadow-room. It came into Jeremy's light, and had the face of a lion, and the face of a bull coming from the lion's cheek. Jeremy held his demon at bay while Maren ripped some moss from off the stone floor. She crept towards the beast, and offered the moss to the bull's mouth, and it snorted. The lion's face licked its lips, and snatched the moss from Maren's hand, narrowly missing her fingers. Jeremy's shield enveloped Maren in an instant.

"That demon isn't necessary," said Maren. Jeremy reluctantly banished it.

The beast then sauntered into the room past Jeremy's energy display and began rolling around in the moss. It seemed to savor every caress of the moss on its back, and then resumed snacking.

Jeremy and Maren started to walk back to the oasis. They opened the door and found Wantoro, Mateo, and Tina on the other side.

"Everything all right?" said Mateo between breaths.

"The torches are back on," said Tina.

"Yep. Take a look at that pussycat." Jeremy sighed, and turned back to see the beast, but it had gone away.

"Did you see it?" asked Tina, taking the moment to dramatically grasp Jeremy's lapel. "I want some action, I'm getting bored. But that was exciting, right?"

"So can I turn off the alarm bells?" asked Wantoro, his eyes landing first on Jeremy, then on Maren.

"Yes," said Maren. "The beast is tame. It was just hungry for moss. I think it's an herbivore. Tell everyone they can rest in peace."

Mateo hesitated. "I don't like it coming so close to the oasis, dear. Really think it was just after the moss?"

"Yeah," said Maren, looking back to where the beast had disappeared. "I'll just make another room for it, try to lead it away. But really, there's nothing to worry about."

Wantoro and Mateo grumbled to one another in some sort of parental understanding and then went back to the root network.

"If it's okay, I'd like to come with," said Tina. "I think I must be like, an adrenaline junkie!"

"More like a Jeremy junkie," mumbled Maren. "Yeah sure, come along."

CHAPTER 36

RED

"That'll do, ladies." Jeremy lay on his back in the third room that Maren had mossed. Somehow the light from the torches brightened with the plants present. "Time to go back." He pointed to the door that they'd come from.

Maren slumped onto the moss. "Like a warm day in June, isn't it?" She lay beside Jeremy.

Tina began to dance by herself, twirling with her arms raised up.

Maren sat up on her elbows. "What was that?" All around them the moss was trembling slightly. Then there was a high-pitched sound coming from the moss, like a little whine.

"Something's not right," said Maren.

Jeremy sighed and got up. "Never should've let my guard down in Mantel's Maze."

They covered their tracks and passed through three uneventful rooms. As they reached the meadow room right before the oasis, Maren broke into a light jog. She passed through the door, circled around the oasis, and then went into the hole that led to the root network. A second later she gasped and clawed her way back up the root lattice. "Move! Move!"

"What?" Jeremy reached down for her and pulled her up, and then he heard a scuttling noise from the hole.

"There's a...!" Maren shook her head, and started to whimper. "Oh God!"

Jeremy took a deep breath and then expanded his energy to form a blue globe around Maren and Tina. "Okay," he said. "I'm going down. I'll keep this shield up, but don't move or I might lose you."

"What!" cried Tina. "What is it!" She yelled at Maren, her voice taking on a new pitch. "Our parents are down there!" Her eyes began to well up.

Jeremy hovered down the passageway into the root network, and his pants caught on a white sticky piece of cotton halfway down the lattice. A web. He heard scuttling in the roots and a dripping sound, and hurried to the bottom, tearing his pants on the web.

An enormous black spider-like creature emerged ten feet away from behind a wall of roots. Its mandibles were the size of machetes, and all around its face were great white whiskers, shiny and thick like snakes. It skittered towards him on hairy legs and spoke in a shrill voice: "True and just are His judgments. Blood eternal will stain all the oceans. It flows!"

Jeremy looked above the spider, and a sac was swinging from the ceiling high above, held up by a single thread. The head of his father hung down, his eyes open, and blood poured forth from his mouth.

"Dad!" Jeremy flew up to him, severing his protective shield from Maren and Tina. He encased his captive father in a blue aura and pulled at the silk binding him, but it would not give. He blasted the thread hanging from the ceiling, but it would not tear.

He looked down on the spider. "What have you done?" He held his palm up and the spider bent its legs. Jeremy sent a large blast at the spider's eight eyes, but it leapt back into the roots and disappeared. "Tell me what you've done!" yelled Jeremy. The spider was above him, scuttling up some vines towards a dark patch on the ceiling.

Jeremy flew twenty feet up. He felt a slight wind. There were four silken ropes coming towards him from all directions, and he reflexively pushed his shield out, but the ropes went right through. In the nick of time, he dropped altitude, and the ropes intertwined in a bundle where he used to be. The ropes were pulled taut, and giant spiders emerged from hollows in nearby root pillars, shimmying down towards him on the ropes, hanging upside down.

The webs were clearly impervious to his powers, but maybe the bodies weren't. Jeremy flew back up the root lattice to the oasis room. "Maren! Tina!" They were gone. He heard a wet hissing right behind him, and he turned to see mandibles poking through the entrance, chomping inches from his face. A snake-whisker lunged at him, snapping taut. Now the legs of the spider were coming through. Jeremy ducked to the side and dodged the hairy, partitioned leg that was coming at him. He darted along the side wall of the oasis room, as more legs came through. The abdomen was too big.

When he was close to the door on the other side, he

held out both hands and fired a series of small blasts towards the spider in a horizontal wave. *One of them will hit.* And sure enough it did, right on the left mandible, which broke in half. The spider shrieked and lunged at Jeremy breaking the stone wall apart and widening the entrance to the oasis. It landed right in the pool, and sank to the bottom.

Jeremy opened the door and closed it behind him. He was in a meadow room. It was empty. Then he noticed that the moss ramped up a few feet towards the left corner.

"Maren, Tina," he whispered. The moss in the corner shook, and Maren and Tina stood up.

"It was pretty cozy in there," said Tina, making a kissy face at Maren. But there were tears in her eyes.

Maren ran to Jeremy, and looked at his face. "Are you okay?"

There was a crash at the wooden door. Jeremy braced his back against it.

"Run away," said Jeremy, and there was another crash against the door.

"No," said Tina.

"Run away, damn it!"

"No, I won't run." Another crash.

Jeremy opened the door immediately after the crash, and blasted the face of a spider who was recoiling. Bits of spider face flew everywhere, and the body slumped in front of them. Another spider leapt over the fallen one and shot a web from its abdomen towards Jeremy. He closed the door and there was a wet slap on the wood. He tried to open the door again, but it was stuck. Try as he might, he couldn't open it. He wiped the sweat off his brow. "Take cover!" Jeremy shouted.

Maren ran towards the back of the room, and Tina reluctantly followed.

Jeremy formed a crackling blue globe in his hands, and pushed the energy into a hard outer shell, which he began to fill with explosive vibrations. He made it denser, and denser. He took a few steps back and aimed it at the corner to the left of the door, and unleashed his power. The globe blasted the wall to pieces, and smoke filled the room. Jeremy flew through the hole, and the room was empty except for the spider carcass and the oasis, bubbling quietly as if nothing had happened. He darted to the enlarged entrance to the root network, and peered into the gloom.

To his horror, the jungle was full of bleeding sacs, the head of his mother, Mateo, Ren, Frisky, General Forero, and everyone else, joining his father.

A dozen spiders emerged from hollows, and then fresh webs criss-crossed around the jungle. For Jeremy, time slowed to a crawl. He saw the webs coming gently towards him, and he swam through the air with ease, adjusting his body into the gaps in the webs. He began to emit walls of energy that were tailored to pass through the webs, and Jeremy blossomed out intricately like an origami sun. Though the spiders leapt away, the energy sought them out, and bits of spider were scattered around the vines like rain.

But the sacs remained, and the blood flowed from the mouths of the people like fountains. Maren and Tina appeared in the entrance to the root network, and screamed at the grotesque display. But the vine lattice was covered in webs, and they couldn't climb down. Jeremy appeared next to them, and brought them to the center of the camp, which had been spared from the shower of spider goo.

"I killed them all. But I can't get my parents down." Jeremy bowed his head.

They all wept for a few moments, but they were interrupted by a loud tap echoing out of the oasis-room. Jeremy, Maren, and Tina looked up just as a long, gnarled tree limb jabbed its way into the hole of the root network.

"Tut, tut," said a voice. "Liverworts." Fedonis the Hermit appeared at the entrance to the oasis room and hopped over the edge, bypassing the vine lattice and landing on a vine bush, which he bounced out of and into a puddle of blood, splashing Maren and Tina.

"They breath still," said Fedonis with one bushy eyebrow up. He helped himself to his feet with his gnarled cane, his sackcloth clothing now even more soiled.

Maren walked up to the hermit in a fury. "Did you just say they're breathing?" She pointed to one of the hanging sacks. "They're dead! Why would they be breathing?" Maren held back her tears. "Speak!"

"Yes," said Fedonis simply.

"Jeremy, try again!" Maren clung to him. "Try again to break the thread. We need to get them out!"

"Tut! It's what I've said and I'll say it again." Fedonis crossed his arms and shook his long white eyebrow hairs fiercely. "A Latin root, it means to protect, to guard, to teach."

Maren faced Fedonis. "Go on."

"Liverworts."

Tina walked over and jabbed a finger at Fedonis. "Out with it already! What are you trying to say you smelly geezer?"

Jeremy constrained her and covered her mouth. "What about liverworts?"

"The spores of the moss have been released." He sniffed. "Never forget a smell." Fedonis cackled and shuffled to the nearest vine tree, and began to climb. He scrambled up towards the ceiling, still holding his cane. He reached over to Wantoro's sac hanging nearby, and tapped it with his cane. Jeremy bristled. "He bleeds from the mouth, and will forever more, until all the oceans and rivers turn red. The ground water will be contaminated. The oasis, too. We will all drink of the blood."

Jeremy shook his head. "Why liverworts?"

"Oh?" Fedonis hopped out of the vine tree and back onto the vine bush, again splashing Maren. He stood up and sniffed in her direction. "It was a sign. I read the sign. And now we'll look for the Mark to confirm, hrm?"

"What mark?" asked Maren.

"The Mark of the Beast," said Fedonis. "There." He pointed to Wantoro's sac. "Go on up then, and have a look. Bunch of ninnies." He grumbled.

They squinted and could see a small mark shining on the sac.

Jeremy grabbed Maren and Tina, and flew up for a look.

χξς

"Some call it Chi Xi Stigma." said Maren. "Other's 666."

"So what then?" interrupted Jeremy. He flew them back down to the muck. "Can we save them?" he asked, staring intently at the hermit.

"Yes, if you lift the Mark."

"Blast it off Jeremy!" cried Tina.

"That won't work, you ninny," said Fedonis. He wagged his finger in her face. "To lift the Mark, you will need to see the duck." He rolled his eyes as if it was obvious.

Maren sighed. "And where is the duck?"

Fedonis looked at her sidelong, a singular eyebrow raised. "Where all the ducks are. They will either say it, or they won't. If it's time, they will say it. If it's not, they will say only, 'Quack.'"

Fedonis turned from them and shambled away towards the back end of the root network. He turned the corner and was gone.

CHAPTER 37

AN OCTAVE HIGHER

They went back through the oasis room, and began to walk through Maren's meadows.

"Let's just find someone, or something." Jeremy pushed the next door open. It was the first room they'd entered without moss. Jeremy stepped through the door. A chandelier twirled majestically overhead, shining kaleidoscope colors across the slick black walls of the cavern. "Beautiful," said Jeremy, and he raised his arms up to savor a feeling of royalty he hadn't had in a long time.

"Guys, there's a crocodile in this room," said Tina, pointing.

A sharp snapping sound made Maren jump and she kicked Jeremy's shin by accident.

"Ouch!" He winced, then laughed. "Whoa, fella." Jeremy held his hands up in peace to the crocodile.

"Hello," said the crocodile in a female voice. She was ten feet away, an easy distance for a croc to cross in a split second.

Maren straightened. "Do you happen to know where any ducks might be?"

"I do," said the crocodile. "But I'm not hungry at the moment." The crocodile snapped and waddled back into the corner of the room.

Jeremy scratched at his chin. "Okay, well could you *tell* us where to find the ducks?"

"Truth is, I'm sad," continued the crocodile. "I suffer from ennui. En-nu-i." The she-croc sniffled, then wailed a soulful wail.

Then Tina began to cry. "You think you've got it bad! You're just a cold-blooded lizard. You have no idea what we've been through."

"What?" snapped the crocodile. "I have clinical depression, you brat. I may not have broken up with some boy-toy, but oh believe me, these tears are real!"

Tina balled her hands into fists.

"Hey," said Jeremy with a leveled hand. "Times are tough. But look at the bright side." He gestured to the lights dappling the walls, and then to the chandelier which twinkled overhead like some majestic disco ball. Jeremy put his hands on his hips. "I think we would all benefit from some interpretative dance."

Maren sighed.

Jeremy marched to the center of the room and faced Maren, Tina, and the crocodile. "When I was younger, I suffered from severe mood swings. My parents tried it all, but I'll tell you—nothing was more therapeutic for me than working out my feelings through a jam session."

Tina stifled a laugh. "I'm feeling a little better already."

"Here, I'll keep the time." Jeremy clapped in time and stomped his heel to make a bass drum. Then he began to hum a sad tune. "Yeah! Let's keep it going."

Tina burst into laughter, and Maren giggled. The crocodile began to tap its tail.

"Yeah, now you're feelin' it! Hum, hum. Now an octave higher—hum, hum! Bring it down, da, da, da, dee. That's up a minor third. Repeat. Hey, let's make it faster!" He kept humming and clapping, and then began to tap dance a funky beat. Now he was whistling a jazz flute solo. The she-crock was wriggling its hips.

"I'm feelin' it, honey!" said the she-crock.

"Just let it go," said Jeremy, and he did a triple front flip while snapping his fingers and keeping up the melody.

"Mmhhmm," said the crocodile.

Tina laughed, and began to shake her butt.

Eventually, Maren shuffled her feet a little.

They jammed for a minute and then faded out.

"All right, feeling better?" asked Jeremy. "How about those ducks?"

The crocodile smiled. "I challenge you to a dance-off, young man."

Jeremy scoffed. "Oh, please. I'm a Danseur noble. I've studied at the Shidz de Ponts Academy of the Fine Arts under Grand Master Ruffle. You have no chance."

"Bring it on then. Girls, give me some space." The crocodile swaggered into the center of the room, and began to tap her tail. Pat, pat, pat, pat. Then she began tapping all sixteen of her claws on the floor like a drum corp. Bbrruptita bruppita bup bup. Brrrrrrupita bruppita bup bup.

"Nice," said Jeremy, nodding his head.

She opened and closed her jaws. Snap. Snap snap.

Snap. Snap snap. The crocodile jumped up on two legs, and whipped its tail around, and the music paused while she launched into the air. She stuck the landing and picked up the beat again. Jeremy was getting a little concerned. But then she goofed, and began to sing off-key in a strained voice. Jeremy shivered a little, and it was over.

"The rhythm work was nice. Could probably work on the vocals. I like to start off with a nice melody, myself," said Jeremy.

The crocodile stepped off stage and Jeremy stepped up. He then began to whistle a jaunty violin line, his hands clasped in front of him, chest out to support his diaphragm. He sang softly and his voice was warm and swelling:

> What pale estate the flittering bird circles,
> Small, wounded, with an exquisite song of pain,
> The cat's bassoon covering it in ecstasy.
> I dug out the roots, the cat mauling bark,
> Loathe, we pulled splinters from our paws.
> The bird, weaning still from the blossom,
> Suckles the air, and
> Falling into a pool,
> Drowns.

He padded lightly across the floor to Maren, pulling her from off the wall, and twirled her. Then he slid forward with both legs bent, released Maren, and sprang into the air with both legs straightened to perfect points. He landed softly and began to chant a strange tune, harmonizing with his own echos around the room. He smiled and brushed his hair off his forehead. He then began to waft around in subtle ballet form, his leading leg changing to fifth position in the air. Jeremy faded the vocals into a hum, still gliding about, when Tina ran to join him on the stage, and he gave her a nasty look. Jeremy announced "pirouette à la seconde," and then twirled on the tip of his right foot, his angelic voice returning with a soaring falsetto, and Jeremy spun faster and faster, creating a wind. His voice climbed higher and higher, reaching the stratosphere. Then he leapt into the air, and there was silence. He floated back down and feigned sleep.

The crocodile clapped her reptilian paws and laughed. "You are a ham, honey." She wiped a tear from her eye. "I've got chills and a big smile."

Jeremy hopped up from off the floor, and bowed several times to his audience. "Thank you. Thank you. Ever since I retired, I always appreciate the opportunity to entertain and enlighten good friends." He dusted himself off and moved beside Maren, who was blushing. Tina snorted.

"Tell you what—I'll give it to you, but only because I'm hungry, sweetheart. All that groovin' gave me an appetite." The crocodile used her teeth to open up a door and then slid on through. "Follow me."

The party travelled through a series of doors, each one opening to a small staircase leading down, down, down.

They passed into an earthen tunnel with a stream running through. The crocodile stopped at the edge of a sloping bank. The she-crock flung her head back, rolling a lizard eye in Jeremy's direction. "Know anything about this?" asked the crocodile with a disgusted look. The water ran red.

"It's just...," Jeremy choked a bit. "It's not what we're looking for."

"Nevermind, the water should be clean further up. That's how the ducks like it," said the crocodile, and she began to waddle off towards the source of the water. Jeremy, Maren, and Tina followed.

The dirt was elevating at a slight angle. They walked beside the stream, occasionally traveling over a stone bridge to the other side to avoid a slippery bank. The water was getting clearer and clearer.

"Sounds delicious," said the crocodile, running up a hill of rocks which created a waterfall. The stream was wider at the top and the ducks were gathered there, swimming against the gentle current. The ducks were multi-colored and their webbed feet were a sparkly gold.

"Quack! Quack!"

The crocodile lunged into the water with the ducks and there was a flurry of quacks and wings as the flock began to rise above the stream. The crocodile leapt out of the water and snapped into a slow duck and brought it down. The rest flew away.

"Hey!" yelled Tina. "We need those ducks!"

"Then go chase 'em," said the crocodile, chewing a wing. "Maybe if you hustled a little, you'd have some dinner too," the crocodile said with a mouth full, and then began to tap off a beat on the bank.

Tina raised her index finger in the air and was about to tell off the crocodile, but Jeremy nudged her forward.

"Thanks," he said. "Come on ladies, if you please." Jeremy picked them up and they each hugged a side of him. He lifted up and raced forward. His pace quickened, and then slowed dramatically.

"We're in the thick of them now," said Jeremy. "Look."

Maren and Tina turned their heads and saw the ducks flying all around them.

"Listen," said Maren.

The ducks seemed to be quacking the word "salmon."

"Salmon?" Tina looked to Maren for confirmation.

"Hold on, ladies." Jeremy veered to the right and set Maren and Tina down. He took off back into the air and snatched a duck by its legs and brought it back to them.

It was flapping multi-colored feathers everywhere. "Quack! Salmon! Quack!" The duck flung its head about.

"Let the poor thing go," said Maren.

Jeremy released the duck and it flew upstream to join the others. "Are there salmon in this stream?"

Maren walked to the water's edge. "A whole school of them."

Tina ran over to the water, and rolled up her sleeves. "Jeremy, don't even think about helping me." She crouched and snatched at a few fish, but they darted away. Then she saw a slow, fat one swimming by, and she pounced on it and held it up victoriously. The fish flapped around.

"Hey salmon," said Jeremy, eyeing the fish up. Its puckered lips gasped for air.

"Put me back in the water!" the fish managed.

Tina lowered the fish back in the water, but didn't

release it. She brought it up again. "All right, now what?"

Maren stepped forward. "Salmon, where are you going?"

"Upstream, to my birth place. Water!"

Tina lowered it again and brought it up.

"Where were you born?" asked Maren.

"The water is so clean and new. The plants are lush." The fish gasped. "Must go back to the garden to die!"

The salmon leapt up from Tina's hands, and came back down and slapped her face with its tail. It splashed into the water and swam away.

"That salmon is saucy!" said Tina.

Maren's eyes widened and she pointed at the stream. "We follow the salmon to the garden."

"Do we really want to go to a garden?" Jeremy sighed. "I know who we'll find there."

"Jeremy, everyone we care about is depending on us. We have no other choice." Maren walked into the swift-moving stream and Tina hopped in and followed her.

"Maren, wait!" Jeremy ran into the water and gripped her by the shoulder. "I have to tell you something."

Maren and Tina stopped and turned around.

"Don't be mad at me for not telling you earlier—but, well I found Lyrna. Lyrna told me why the spirit animals are attacking people. They are trying to extract the soul because everyone is already dead."

Maren just stared at him.

"What do you mean, 'everyone is already dead?' I feel fine." Tina frowned at Jeremy.

"Ever since the Apocalypse started, the dead haven't been passing through the Haze. And then the Haze collapsed into this world. No one can survive for long in the Haze, except for me." Jeremy stared at the ground. "The spirit animals are here for the sorting."

"So... we're dead, and so are our parents? Is it all in vain?" asked Maren. She watched the salmon leap.

Jeremy drew a deep breath. "I don't know for sure." He frowned. "We'd have to bring Lyrna down here to find out. If she claws at you, she's only trying to sort you."

"Don't bring her!" said Tina. Her cheeks reddened and tears dripped down her cheeks and into the stream. "I need a drink."

Jeremy leaned in and hugged Maren and Tina. "Fedonis told us that we can save our families from the webs. But we can't bring them back to life. We have to help them." Jeremy knelt down in front of Maren and kissed her belly. "He's still kicking, right?"

"Yes," said Maren. "And growing too, by the looks of it."

Jeremy tried his best to smile at her. "Time's sped up."

The sound of the flowing stream should have been peaceful, but instead the splashes of the salmon as they leapt and swam back to their birth place to die made it seem a dreadful place.

"We have to go to the garden then," said Maren at last. She lay her hands on her belly and looked upstream.

"We're going to Mantel," said Jeremy.

"It's where we're supposed to be," said Maren.

CHAPTER 38

RETURN TO THE GARDEN

It took several hours to make their way through the dirt tunnel, wading upstream against the current. The tunnel finally opened up into a bright cavern with a small bay. A shoreline with a white sandy beach lay across the water, and beyond that there was a thicket of fruits and vegetables. Jeremy had refused to assist Maren and Tina and hasten their journey. He wanted them to feel each moment—the sloshing of the water, the slap of the salmon on their thighs. Each sensation felt more and more precious the closer they came to the garden. Who knew what the Apocalypse had in store for them.

Maren was the first to step onto the shore. Mantel's garden stretched as far as the eye could see, with tidy columns of white stone punctuating the vastness, joining the cavity in the earth to the bedrock that separated the mantel from the crust. The place was well-lit by torches arranged on the ceiling. Rows upon rows of vegetables and low-lying fruit lay before them. Jeremy and Tina stepped ashore, and they crept down a row of eggplants and into a patch of watermelons. Soon, they met some spinach.

Maren stooped and pulled off some leaves. She ate it in silence, and Jeremy and Tina joined her.

"Mantel's Garden is supposed to tell us how to bring our family back," said Maren. "If we're all dead, I suppose it's not so bad to live, er, to be dead like this." She lifted up her arm and examined it.

"Sounds like something Mantel would say," said Jeremy.

They moved further inland, until at last the sloshing of the water on the bank disappeared. "There are so many torches here," said Maren. "But nothing can replace the sun. How can these plants grow?"

Jeremy shrugged. "Hey, look over there." He pointed to a nearby column that had a subtle outline of a door.

"How did you even see that?" asked Tina, squinting at the stone.

"Let's go in," said Maren.

Jeremy held up his hand. "After we rest."

Maren and Tina saw the wisdom in that, and quietly arranged a bed of lettuce. They lay on it, fidgeting for a time, and finally fell asleep.

Tina was the first to wake up, and she nudged the two lovers with the tip of her purple moccasin. Jeremy and Maren rolled over and their eyes fluttered open: Tina had set a small pile of berries, carrots, and peaches in front of them.

"Thanks," said Jeremy, and he picked up a peach. Maren did the same. Tina nibbled on a carrot. After they'd finished, they threw their scraps into the distance (it was all a compost heap, anyway) and faced the fated door.

Maren approached the column and Jeremy nudged the door open. "It's clear," he said. Tina stared wistfully back in the direction of the stream, and Maren had to pull her forward.

They tiptoed in and walked through a dim, rectangular room with a door on the other side. Jeremy eased the door open. It was Mantel's banquet room. In the middle of the room were two long silver tables set with silver cutlery, and a large crystal chandelier hung from the ceiling. Towards the back end was a gold statue depicting a harvest scene. The room was lined with huge plants, and smelled like rose water. In one corner was a fountain and there were three doors. What seemed like so long ago, they were sitting at the table when a horde of monsters ambushed them and burst through the door. "I wonder what ever happened to ol' Serious Steven," mumbled Jeremy. He looked at Maren.

"Let's just have a seat."

"Yeah, let's just redo what happened last time, sounds like a plan. Or we could leave!" said Tina, crossing her arms.

Just then, they heard heavy footsteps outside the door by the statute. They all dove behind massive potted plants, and the door swung open. Ms. Fritz and an entourage of ogre-like creatures walked in. The ogres stood by the doorway while Ms. Fritz lifted a golden goblet off the table and made for the fountain in the corner. She filled up the cup and set it down in the middle of a table, and then left the room, ogres in tow.

When they were gone for a minute, Tina stuck her head out of the leaves and gestured to Jeremy and Maren. But they heard footsteps again.

The door swung open, and Mantel hovered into the room in a long black cloak. He looked like a pink frog with stunted appendages, and his skin was a flowing membrane, faces bubbling to the surface and then receding. He raised an arm in the direction of the golden goblet. Black smoke gathered around him, intermingling with his black cloak brushing on the floor. Ms. Fritz followed, careful not to step on his cloak, and Jasmine behind her, carrying her baby. The goons followed, and then these were followed by a whole host of characters. A crowd gathered around the tables, and Mantel took a seat at the head. Jeremy and Maren watched the scene unfold from behind the bush. Standing right in front of the bush, facing away from them was Serious Steven—their one-time mysterious camping buddy long ago. His Reeboks were extra white, as if polished for an auspicious event.

"Bring me my bowl," croaked Mantel from his throne.

Ms. Fritz disappeared behind another door and returned with a cart of fresh vegetables. She wore gloves that glistened all the way up to her elbows, and began to load an orange clay bowl with squash, eggplants, tomatoes, and bell peppers. When the bowl was full, she strode over to Mantel and placed the bowl in front of him. She bowed and then took her seat beside him. The seat on his other side remained empty. Then servants with carts of vegetable dishes wheeled the feast into the room, and set it on the table.

"Where is he?" asked Mantel.

"He should be here soon," said Jasmine in reassuring tones.

There was a sneeze behind a shrub, followed by a terse "damn it!"

Jeremy squeezed Maren's knee. They were about to discover Tina.

"How interesting," said Mantel, turning to the potted plant ten feet away in the corner of the room.

Just then, an old man with a cane hobbled out from behind one of the plants, and approached the table, mumbling to himself. He was wearing his finest sackcloth. "Ten paces, then turn, another forty? Forty-seven, I believe. That should have brought me—"

"Fedonis!" said Ms. Fritz. "Have a seat."

Fedonis paused, and raised his bushy white eyebrows. "Aha! Tut, tut." He shuffled over and sat at Mantel's right.

"Fedonis shall have the parsley soup," said Mantel, nodding to Ms. Fritz.

"Should I then? Hrm, I'll be the boss of my own soup, I should think." Fedonis was cleaning his ear with one pinky.

"Sire," began Ms. Fritz, "should we say a few words?"

"No!" Mantel lay his hand on a squash and brought it up to his pink, bubbly lips. "We eat in silence." He bit into the flesh of the squash.

Everyone in the room sat down at the tables, and began to eat in silence, save the ogres and Fedonis, who chewed with their mouths open.

Everyone ate their fill, and then waited in silence as

Mantel continued to eat. Fedonis belched, and then Ms. Fritz snuffed with displeasure. At last, Mantel set his fork down and took one last, long swig from his golden goblet. He set it down. "You may come out now, Jeremy Chikalto."

Jeremy laughed to himself and emerged from behind the tall, leafy plant. "Hello, Mantel. Fedonis."

"Apollyon, you're late to dinner," replied Fedonis. He patted his belly. "It was a good one, shouldn't have any problems in the old piping." Fedonis patted Mantel on what might have been a shoulder and stood up with his cane. He hobbled over to Jeremy, who was quite tense and beginning to glow an electric blue.

"Is this a betrayal?" said Jeremy.

The old man squinted at him and leaned in. "No, just a prophecy." He winked, and then made for the exit. "I'm through here," he said, waving his hand behind him. "I'd like some peace and quiet now, if you don't mind. Rapscallions." The door closed behind him with a forceful thud, and Jeremy faced Mantel.

"Yes?" asked Jeremy.

Mantel floated up from his seat.

"I invite your friends to join me as well. Tina? Maren?"

Tina hopped out from behind her plant and crossed her arms.

Maren stepped into view as well.

"Maren Nononia," said Mantel with relish. Jeremy flashed and was beside Maren. Tina joined them. He formed a dome around them and sent a few rings of sparks into the room. A couple of Mantel's party guests yelped.

"If you test me, you will regret it," said Jeremy.

Mantel's guests began to edge away from Jeremy.

"But what comes next?" asked Mantel. "I've wondered for centuries. The prophesied birth of Apollyon from the line of the fallen angel Vordin. The boy who sees behind the air. And what now?" Mantel looked at Maren. "My Maze speaks to you, I know. What does it say?" Mantel drifted closer to the globe and black smoke wisped around him. "You have a halo, I see."

Maren was beginning to emit a soft white light from her crown.

"What?" Jeremy reached out to touch it and the halo disappeared.

Mantel's eyes bulged at Maren. "Why do the plants serve you? What does the Maze want with your baby? I created everything in here. I am the lord of this realm."

Jeremy's eyes flashed. "You won't touch a hair on her head. Now that the Haze has collapsed, I am more powerful than you can imagine."

Mantel laughed. "No need for strong words, we were merely germinating an idea." He lifted his small, fetal-like hand: in it was a single bean.

"What's that?" asked Jeremy.

"I trust that your reflexes have improved." Mantel dropped the bean and all the light left the room. Mantel's banquet guests panicked and fled the room, the ogres stomping through the crowd, and knocking Serious Steven aside. The various odds and ends of creature-people managed to squeeze out, but Ms. Fritz remained behind, a firm hand wrapped around Jasmine's wrist. Jasmine, the stronger of the two, stood by Ms. Fritz, holding her baby in her other arm, powerless.

Jeremy lit up the room with a blue light. It was reflected back to him at a hundred different angles. "Mirrors?"

"You could say that," said a disembodied voice.

The room was now a mirror maze, and Jeremy, Maren, and Tina were partitioned off in a small, reflective hallway.

"I can blow this place apart in a matter of seconds," said Jeremy.

"Try it and see what happens. Every shard is the ashes of a cruel soul, burned to glass." Mantel coughed, and something large slithered out of his wet mouth.

"What do you want from us?" asked Maren.

There was a shuffling from somewhere within the mirrored walls.

"Our work has not been in vain, my loyal ones," said Mantel.

Ms. Fritz and Jasmine cried out, fearing the end was near.

"I have enriched the soil—and now the baby will flourish. Maren carries the seed. "

"Mantel? What do you mean?" whispered Ms. Fritz.

"Be at peace, my servant. Apollyon will call out his demons, and we will test his worth," said Mantel. The reflective surfaces of the mirrors shimmered, and Jeremy saw two faces of Mantel, one enraged, and one placid. All at once, the mirrors vanished. Ms. Fritz and Jasmine were bound together and sitting back to back in the center of the room. Jasmine's baby was on her lap.

Mantel floated above them, dripping a pink ooze and gagging on something in his throat. "It's the demon trace, Apollyon. Your spirit animals crave it too, and will come to the Maze. The soul will flee, but must be caught in the end, caught in the great tide."

"Don't hurt them, they have given everything for you," said Maren.

"Yes, they have given themselves over. Everything must give itself over, everything must yield. The buds spout from the wet ground in the spring, grow tall in the hot summer, and bear fruit in autumn. Come winter, they shrivel to the ground." Mantel smiled at Maren. "I see you now, Maren Nononia, for what you bring forth. As for you Jeremy, call on your demons, or I will spill this mother's blood and summon them myself."

Jasmine's baby began to cry.

Jeremy shot a ripple of blue energy up through the ceiling.

A sound like an angry hive of bees began vibrating through the banquet hall, and the room darkened. Shadows with outstretched hands began to gather in the corners of the room. A demon with the head of a goat stepped towards Mantel. It opened its mouth, and a great wind began to suck through the room.

"Mantel!" Maren called out, and she stepped outside of Jeremy's protective barrier. He was so focused on keeping things out, he never thought to keep things in. Mantel flickered and appeared in front of Maren, and she reached out to him and touched the mark on his neck. The mark spoke to her in strange words, much like the army of demons chattering in the corners. Maren hesitated.

"You touch my curse," said Mantel with a gruesome smile. "Is that what you were looking for?"

"Nisi," she said, reading the Latin inscription. "Except, only...?

"Yes," he replied.

Jeremy's energy globe reformed around Maren, and he blasted Mantel to the ground, burning away the cloak to expose the shriveled, pink form. Mantel rose again into the air, naked with knobby limbs pushing out of his gut. His body began to swell, his skin growing thin like a horrible balloon, and faces inside him wailed and pressed against skin, gnawing to break free.

Jeremy unleashed the demons onto Mantel, and they swarmed him like bees from a broken hive. Jeremy relocated Maren and Tina to the corner of the room. As the demons tore into the bloated Mantel, and the souls inside him raged against their prison, the ceiling began to shake, and large chucks of stone fell to the floor, releasing beams of torchlight into the room from above.

Jeremy, Maren, and Tina watched from inside the safety of Jeremy's fortress.

"It's time to leave, Jeremy," said Maren with a frown.

But Jeremy wasn't leaving yet. Beads of sweat rolled down his face, and he felt the ecstasy of the demons doing their work.

"There's one last loose end to tie up," he said. Then out of the chaos, a lone demon drifted through the membrane of energy surrounding them, and approached

Jeremy. Maren and Tina gasped and recoiled. The demon was skeletal and clothed in black rags. It had the face of a boy. Jeremy and the demon merged together, and its darkness receded into his body. Then his chest glowed red. Maren and Tina watched in horror.

Jeremy summoned more demons, and what was left of Mantel shot up through a hole in the ceiling, the demons flowing after him in a black stream. Across the room, huddled under the banquet table and the rubble were Ms. Fritz, Jasmine, and Jasmine's baby.

"Let's get them and go, now's our chance!" Maren tried to run over to them, but couldn't get through Jeremy's energy barrier this time.

Jeremy called out across the room. "Jasmine, you and your baby may join us."

Jasmine crawled out from under the table with a wailing baby, and dashed across the room and into Jeremy's protective globe. Just then Mantel's body crashed back into the room, and the demons poured in after him.

"But what about you, what do you deserve?" asked Jeremy as Ms. Fritz crawled out from under the banquet table. Mantel was battling the demons in the corner.

Jeremy left his globe around Maren, Tina, Jasmine, and the baby, and flashed over to Ms. Fritz and picked her up by the throat.

"Jeremy!" cried Maren, pressing against the wall of Jeremy's energy. "Are you out of your mind? Get us out of here!"

"Have a nice view, Gorda?" said Jeremy, nodding in the direction of Mantel and the swarm of demons.

Ms. Fritz's eyes bulged and she flailed in Jeremy's grasp. He threw her to the floor and kicked her in the ribs.

"Jeremy, stop!" yelled Maren.

"This woman took me from my parents when I was a child. It's only right that she suffers now." Another demon swam into Jeremy, and another. Jeremy grabbed Ms. Fritz's hand and pulled a finger from its socket. He laughed as she screamed in pain.

Jeremy ignored his friends, and the globe of energy imprisoning them shimmered and weakened. Tina burst through the barrier and ran over to Jeremy. She grabbed him just as he reached for another of Ms. Fritz's fingers. Another demon flew into him, and his eyes flashed at Tina.

"This is none of your concern," he barked.

"Don't hurt her."

Jeremy swatted Tina aside. He seized Ms. Fritz once more, this time twisting her arm behind her until it popped.

Tina got up and jumped on his back, biting his shoulder with all her might, and he flung her down again.

"Stay out of this unless you want the same," he yelled.

"This isn't you anymore!" shouted Tina, baring her teeth.

Jeremy glared back at her, breathing hard. He reformed his protective shield.

"The demons are in you," she said.

"They always have been."

The banquet room was a war zone of crumbled stone splattered with Mantel's slime. The demons in a frenzy in the corner, and still Mantel fought them. He cast them off with a deafening blast, and demons were scattered everywhere. Mantel rose into the air again, and the pink ooze painting the room began to bubble, and all the pieces of Mantel gathered back into him like a reverse explosion. Mantel floated into the center of the cavern.

"I give myself over, and you want revenge? You are not worthy of my submission, Apollyon. Leave Gorda alone. End this, *now*."

Jeremy burst into a white flame, and Mantel pushed all of his darkness out, and the two forces met in the middle, and spread out in all directions. The demons swarmed together at the edge of Jeremy's energy, and then burst into Mantel's darkness. Jeremy summoned more demons, which flew like dark spears through Jeremy's white aura and into Mantel. Finally, all the demons inside him shot out to join the mass. Jeremy closed his energy around the darkness, and compacted it like a black hole.

And Mantel was torn into a thousand shreds, all screaming in agony. The demons' work almost complete, they sucked each fragment in, and the mass turned a fiery red as Hell reclaimed its children. There was silence, and the demons dispersed from the room. Jeremy's light faded.

A single strand of Mantel inched along the floor towards Jeremy's feet like a worm. Jeremy raised his foot over top of it to stomp it, but then he heard Ms. Fritz cry. He turned to her and then a great "Mew!" came from overhead and Lyrna flew down from the blasted hole in the upper level of the banquet hall and past them, brushing Maren's shoulder. The fizdruft swooped down on the fragment of Cain, and took it gently in her teeth. She swam upward, and the fragment glowed white and illuminated the room. Lyrna disappeared again into the hole in the ceiling and the cavern felt empty.

CHAPTER 39

THE MARK

The banquet hall had been stripped of its former glory and utterly demolished. Even the torchlights, with their ethereal flames, had been extinguished. A small amount of light trickled into the banquet room from some far-away chamber above. Yet it seemed that a lightness hung about the place. Jeremy, Maren, and Tina clustered together, and Maren extended a hand to Ms. Fritz and Jasmine. Ms. Fritz, still shaking in pain and heartache, accepted. Jasmine did the same.

"A small part of Mantel still wanted to go back to the One. It wanted to yield, to be redeemed," said Maren. She turned to Jeremy. "Nisi." She pointed to her neck. "I saw the Mark of Cain on his neck. I think it's the spell to lift the Mark of the Beast. Let's get back to the others—I have an idea."

They made their way back to their friends and family mummified in spider webs hanging from the ceiling of the root network. As they approached the door to the oasis chamber, the smell of iron was strong—blood. Jeremy nudged the door open and they could see that the blood was pooling deep on the ground.

Before heading down into the root network, Jeremy

reluctantly popped Ms. Fritz's arm back into place at Maren's request. After the procedure, Jeremy ferried them to the ground below, and they were knee deep in a dark red blood, almost brown, and thick clots were forming everywhere.

"Hold on," said Jeremy, and he waded through the blood a short distance and then blasted the ground with a controlled beam of energy. The blood sprayed, and then drained into the deep hole he'd created.

"Thanks, I think," said Tina, wiping the drops of blood off her face.

"Let's do this." Jeremy stared up at the sacs illuminated by torch light from the oasis room and the dull glow of the root network.

"All right Maren, what now?"

"The Mark of Cain is the spell to lift the curse of the Mark of the Beast."

"What if it just makes things worse? What if it's just another one of Mantel's tricks?" asked Tina. Ms. Fritz scowled.

"How would we know the difference?" said Jeremy.

Maren shook her head. "Wisdom is proved right by her children. Jeremy, fly me up to your dad, and you'll see."

Jeremy paused. "I trust Maren," he said finally. He wrapped his arms around her, and they hovered up to the sac.

"Nisi," said Maren as she ran her fingers over the Mark.

χξς

213

"Nisi!" she repeated. Nothing.

They set up camp as best they could next to the oasis. Despair was beginning to set in, and they were exhausted.

"I'm going to lay down for a while," said Maren, and she retreated to a mat of moss in the corner. Her mind drifted as she lay on the moss, and soon she fell asleep.

There was a temple made of wood, and two men approached with offerings in their arms. One man approached with the fruit of his harvest, and the other with a slain lamb. They placed the offerings on a stone altar in the temple, and sat on the ground, their heads bowed in prayer.

After a time, the gardener spoke to the shepherd. "Brother, I have labored this whole year in the dirt, and look what I have grown. From my sweat have I brought this gift for the Lord, without spilling a drop of blood except my own. You have laid in the field while the animals eat the grass, and slept under the sun, and then you slew this lamb today. Who do you think has done right by the Lord?"

And the shepherd was saddened by these words. "Brother, I have done only as the Lord has asked me to do. We are the same."

"We are not the same!" Mantel's will burned in Cain's eyes. "Because my offering to the Lord is greater, so the Lord's love for me will be greater."

And the Lord, who was always watching from the unseen place, spoke to the men as they sat. "If you offer properly, but divide improperly, have you not sinned?"

And then the scene swirled, and she saw Mantel in his Maze for thousands of years, alone but surrounded by souls. Mantel looked at her through the dream. "Except," he said. "I tried to be apart, to become an exception. But everyone, always, belongs to the One. This, now, I accept."

Maren awoke and left her hut to join the others, who were sitting at the edge of the oasis room looking down at the root network and telling stories about the old days. They turned to look at Maren.

"When we found the salmon they said to us, 'We have to return to our birth place to die.' All forms are born out of the One, and all must return to the One, which is always forming and unforming."

"Death," said Jeremy.

"No, true death is when you refuse to go back. Cain's Mark—Nisi. It means 'except, only.' Accept." said Maren.

"Accept," she said again and again, and the air began to vibrate with the word. The halo around Maren's crown appeared again and began to shine like a beacon. Maren felt like a pool of water expanding, submerging the Maze, and it seeped through the webs, and she could feel her friends and family raging in their prisons. She vibrated into them: *Accept*. And their minds grew calm and still like a cup holding the water.

"Look!" Jeremy grabbed Maren and Tina and flew them down into the root network. "The thread is unravelling!"

The blood had stopped pouring out of Wantoro's

mouth, and he was unleashed from the sac into Jeremy's arms waiting below. Jeremy eased him onto the ground, and Wantoro's limbs began to convulse. Soon he was coughing up blood from his lungs. He opened his eyes and looked around him.

Jeremy grabbed hold of his father's face and kissed him. "You're alive!"

"I'm dead," said Wantoro, with a smile slowly spreading across his face.

Maren knelt down beside him and clasped his hand. "I think we all are."

CHAPTER 40

BATHED IN LIGHT

One by one, the prisoners were released from the sacs and revived, and there were many joyous reunions. Jeremy and Maren moved everyone into the oasis room and away from the blood. Then Jeremy dismantled the spider carcass in the oasis bit by bit, and threw the remains into the roots. He blasted the pool again and again, hoping to sterilize it, if that even meant anything anymore.

"How are you feeling?" Maren crouched beside her father.

Mateo smiled up at her. "I'm okay. When I was strung up like a sausage, all I could think about was my girls. You, your mother... your baby."

Maren laughed. "A girl, huh?"

Mateo smiled. "Just a hunch. Your mother was calling to me." The corners of Mateo's eyes welled up. "I think we all felt it, Maren. It's time to leave."

"Yeah." Maren walked to the other side of the oasis room and stood beside Jeremy. She faced the group and cleared her throat. A hush spread across the room.

"I'm amazed that people can go through an experience like yours and be grateful for it. I have something to tell everyone. We know why the spirit animals are attacking us." She took a deep breath. "It's because we're all already dead. After the Apocalypse began, the world of spirits merged with our own. Everyone on this plane has died, but our spirits haven't yet been... processed. The spirit animals separate our energies. A part of us goes up, and a part of us goes down. Jeremy has control over the demons, and they will do us no harm. But he does not control the spirit animals. You control the spirit animals." Maren smiled. "The good news is that you can all be sorted peacefully. The spirit animals only fight the body that resists the sorting. I propose we bring the spirit animals to us. We let them take us!"

There was a pregnant silence.

"You're right," said Frisky. "While I was in the sac, I knew it with all my being that I wanted to be someplace else. I saw my parents, grams, relatives I'd only ever heard stories about. I'm not afraid." She reached out to Ren, and he smiled at her.

Jeremy pulled Maren aside. "What are you doing?" he whispered.

"Don't you hear them? It's what they want."

"Is it what you want?"

Maren looked back at her father, who was reclining on the moss, his face bathed in light. "I think so."

Tina wedged herself between them. "I think I can do this!" She laughed, wiped away a stray tear and then ran over to her parents.

"They're actually celebrating," said Jeremy under his breath.

Maren rubbed her temples. "I think I need another nap," she said.

"Yeah, well me too." Jeremy opened a door up to the next room over. It was a simple, rectangular room carpeted in moss with four torches burning in each of the four corners. "We're all exhausted. Let's sleep on it and then decide."

CHAPTER 41

IT ROAMS

Something fell on Jeremy's nose. He swiped it away, but then another flake fell into the crease of his eye, and he reflexively batted his eyelash. This woke him. "Hey, Maren?" Jeremy nudged her softly and then moved away from the wall where he'd been resting. He looked up and saw that the ceiling was crumbling slightly just above them. "Maren!"

She was roused from her sleep, and rubbed at her eyes. Dust and debris settled on her head. "What is this?" Maren scooched beside Jeremy.

"The ceiling is falling," said Jeremy.

"Look over there," said Maren, pointing. A crack was spreading to the other side of the room, growing thicker with each passing second.

"We should check out the graveyard. Maybe Mantel's fight with the demons destabilized the infrastructure of the Maze."

"Right." Maren stretched her arms overhead and then made for the door. "Let's keep this to ourselves for the time being."

Jeremy and Maren walked by the others, who were talking to one another about the sorting and visions that they had about life beyond. Jeremy carried Maren as he flew through the root network, still bloodied and with webs strung up, criss-crossing every which way, until they ascended into the graveyard passageway.

The graveyard was ill lit where they stood.

"Go towards the torch light," said Maren.

They passed row after row of gravestones and came to a pile of debris from Earth's surface. A small stream of dirt fell on top of his head and Jeremy frantically styled the dust out of his hair. He jumped off the pile of debris, but was too late—his weight had already caused more damage. "It's bad."

They looked at the ceiling of the Maze. "You think...?"

"The Earth is collapsing in on itself." Maren gasped. "We have to sort everyone, now."

Jeremy stopped short and studied a spot in the distance. "Do you see that?"

"What?" Maren squinted.

"Something's coming," whispered Jeremy. "It's flying towards us."

"What?" She looked where Jeremy had pointed and could detect a small movement. Something airy fluttered towards them. It shined like gold. As it drew closer, it whispered, "Apollyon."

Jeremy stepped towards it. "Did you hear that?"

"Be careful," said Maren.

Jeremy held up a cautious hand. It floated closer and then stopped mid-air. All he had to do was grab it. It was a key.

Maren gasped. "Jeremy, don't!"

"It's a key," he looked back at Maren. "Does that mean...?"

Maren's face lost all its color.

"I'm not the Antichrist." Jeremy laughed. "I can't be, right? If I take this key—so what, I'd lock myself away? No."

"I never thought you were," she said.

"I wasn't sure, but I should take this right now, right?" His smile was manic, but she remained stoic. "Maren, what should I do?"

"Leave it."

Jeremy blinked. "I can't just leave it."

"You can get it later. Please." Maren gripped him by the arms. "We need everyone sorted before you get that key. Bring me back to everyone and I'll tell them to prepare. You find Lyrna."

* * *

Jeremy stood on Earth's surface. Earth had grown hot —very hot—and the red sun beat down without mercy. An earthquake shook the ground beneath his feet slightly. All around him the structures and trees were decimated by fire and powerlines were toppled by storms.

Jeremy took to the sky. "Lyrna!" he called out. Thousands of spirit animals clustered around him, demons too, all eager for him to call them to some end. He closed his eyes and focused his attention on Lyrna.

Jason. The thought pierced his brain. What did it all matter, anyway? If Maren was already dead—if his parents, Mateo, Tina, Frisky, and Ren were all already dead—what was the rush to have them sorted? Mantel's vision of individuated souls living forever in the Maze seemed more tempting than ever.

Jason. The thought resurfaced and made him sick. So he killed a young boy—it was the boy's gun.

With newfound alacrity, Jeremy made it to the Truitt house in Pennsylvania in minutes. The sun and moon spun past in quick succession, a strobe light in the sky. He was soon soaring above the Endless Mountains in western Pennsylvania. *Make this quick*, he thought to himself. He was supposed to be finding Lyrna.

Jeremy approached the property slowly. The trees had long since burned away, replaced now by ashes and dirt. When he reached the top of the once tree-lined hill, he saw the house and it looked just like he'd left it. The porch was erected on stodgy wooden stilts set in a cement foundation. Outside carpet, worn by the elements, nonetheless remained intact on the steps leading up to the front door. And the shed that served as Jeremy's prison looked every bit the nightmare from his youth.

A young man walked out the front door holding a rake and a large bucket. He continued down the porch steps and made his way to the center of the yard. Jeremy hid behind the shed. The young man raked the dirt into the bucket until it was full. *Jason.* But it couldn't be, he'd killed Jason. Jeremy's heart beat in his chest. "Jason?"

The young man stood upright. "Hello?"

"Are you Jason?" Jeremy emerged from behind the shed.

"No. I'm sorry, he died some time ago."

Jeremy stopped and drew a sharp breath. "I was a friend of his. Forgive me, but you look so much like him."

"He was my brother."

Jeremy nodded stupidly. "Of course," he said.

"Yeah. I've been here about three years. How did you know my brother? Why are you here? Lookin' for refuge?"

Jeremy stammered.

"Hey, it's okay. We make due here. You wouldn't believe it, but we've been eating the dirt all this time—it must be loaded with nutrients. Hey, we'd love to have a friend of Jason's!"

Jeremy began to break into a sweat. "I'd better not come in." He held his hands up in deference. "But your brother was great. He, um, was fiercely loyal. I heard he knew right away that Jacey Moon wasn't you. He just..." Jeremy struggled to find the words, "Jason knew something wasn't right, so the gun... it's just a shame how that all went down."

"You look familiar now that I see you up close." Jeffrey squinted.

Jeremy froze, unsure whether to bolt or to beg for forgiveness. He so desperately wanted closure. "I'd better go—"

"Jacey Moon," said Jeffrey.

"Yes," said Jeremy, still as stone. "My name's Jeremy Chikalto, actually."

Jeffrey knelt down and picked up the bucket of dirt.

"I just wanted to apologize."

After a pause, Jeffrey had the courage to speak. "Is it

true you're the Antichrist?"

Jeremy stiffened. "I have a role to play in the Apocalypse, but I'm not the Antichrist."

Jeffrey grabbed the rake and pathetically held it up to protect himself. "Get out of here. Please," he said.

"I'm not going to hurt anyone," said Jeremy. "The spirit animals that fly overhead will come for you, but don't be afraid. There is a... Heaven. Have peace." Jeremy hesitated, took a couple of steps back, and then glowed an electric blue. He turned and saw Lyrna floating in the air just behind him.

"Meow!"

"Lyrna! Thank God," said Jeremy.

She started to growl and flexed her claws. "It roams," said Lyrna.

"Come with me." Jeremy grabbed her by the scruff of the neck and flew up into the sky, leaving Jeffrey stupefied.

CHAPTER 42

THE SORTING

When Jeremy returned to the Maze, he found ghosts and amalgamated soul-creatures circled around Maren. She had Mantel's scepter—an onyx rod with gold foil cornucopia embellishments—on her lap in a gesture of good will. "I guess I started a movement," said Maren when she saw him.

"I've got Lyrna." Jeremy gestured to the next room over. "What's going on?"

Maren stood up and brushed the dirt off of her butt. "Ms. Fritz and Jasmine have been out spreading the word that Mantel's been sorted. Many of these souls have been in the Maze so long that they're actually relieved to go too."

Jeremy fidgeted.

"Tina has volunteered to be the first one to be sorted." Maren called Tina over to her, who was standing a few feet away, and she held Tina's hands.

"We'd like to be sorted at the same time," said General Forero and Tina's mother, Anna, stepping past the creatures to join them.

"Of course." Maren smiled at Tina's family.

Jeremy frowned and a flake of dirt crumbled from the ceiling and fell on his nose.

"What was that?" asked Tina, leaning towards Jeremy to investigate.

"Nothing," Jeremy drew back from her.

"I want everyone to see me go," said Tina. "Not only because I'm fabulous, but so everyone can see that it's going to be okay. If Maren's right—if I've accepted my death—than Lyrna will sort me peacefully." Tina continued, her eyes wide and inviting, "I believe in Maren, and I believe in you too, Jeremy. I know what's on the other side. Bliss, memories, and more—a future."

Maren reached out for Jeremy's hand. "Let's say goodbye," she said.

"Okay?" Jeremy frowned.

"Stay strong, Jeremy," she whispered.

"Tina, can I talk with you for a second?" Jeremy tried to mask his emotions, but was never very good at self-restraint. He pulled her away from her family and whispered, "Are you sure you want to go first? You're ready?"

"Yes."

"Because...? I'm sorry, but...that's it—you're ready to just go?"

Tina laughed. "Well, I'd love to see you fight the Antichrist, don't get me wrong. But I'm in way over my head. This is all you, Jeremy. Plus, I'm dead!" She shrugged. "I'll see you soon. Can you flex for me real quick?"

Jeremy winced. "How are you even thinking about something like that?"

Tina crossed her arms.

Jeremy looked over his shoulder, saw that nobody was paying attention, and then produced a muscle for Tina, which she gleefully wrapped her hands around.

"Ooo la la!" She winked. "Better get back to my parents. Punch Satan in the face for me." Tina patted Jeremy on the shoulders. And then she gave Jeremy a pity hug.

It was the first time he'd been on the receiving end of a pity hug. "Okay," he said, wiping a tear from his eye. "Let me go and get Lyrna."

Jeremy wanted to take his time retrieving his fizdruft, but the floor shook slightly and some more debris crumbled from the ceiling. He opened the door to Lyrna's chamber. "Lyrna, we need you over here. Be gentle." He wiped at his brow. This was really happening. He admired Tina's readiness, but couldn't accept it. She was always braver than him.

Jeremy and Lyrna entered the room shielded from the onlookers by a large force field. Everyone stood along the back of the wall for the viewing. Jeremy reached out and pulled Tina into the force field, followed by General Forero and Anna.

"Hi, Lyrna," said Tina, and she lay down on the floor. Her parents followed suit.

Lyrna fluffed her fur out a little and stretched out her claws.

Jeremy eyed his fizdruft suspiciously. "Gentle, Lyrna. Everyone, make yourself like water. Slow down your breathing. Be at peace."

Everyone quieted down and Tina giggled. Jeremy

couldn't help but admire her. Lyrna padded forward.

"Mew!" She purred.

"Love you, mom and dad."

"Love you too, Tina."

Lyrna swept her paw at Tina's sternum and caught hold of a wispy chord. She pulled it forward and Tina quieted. Tina's body lay still, but her spirit swam upward with Lyrna. She waved at everyone with an ethereal hand and her physical body shimmered and was no more. Lyrna did the same to General Forero and Anna, until she held three chords in her mouth. Then the pilot and her passengers disappeared.

Everyone cheered. Jeremy had to turn away to prevent the others from seeing his tears. His chest tightened.

Maren appeared behind him and placed a gentle hand on his shoulder. "Don't let them see you this way," she whispered.

The remaining party broke into separate groups—those who wished for a public sorting, and those who opted for a private sorting. The public sortings were granted first. One by one, they shimmered from existence on this plane. Mateo opted for a grand exit and requested a last dance with Maren. He looked as merry as ever. "Hope to meet my grandchild soon—I love you both!" Jeremy pulled Mateo into the ring, and Mateo shook his hand with gusto. "I'm going to see my wife again. Lyrna, take me dancing." Everyone cheered Mateo on and Lyrna floated over his chest and pulled his spirit free. He shimmered and disappeared.

Jeremy had to take a break. He led Lyrna to her

private chamber, and then flew off into a separate room and balled his eyes out. Why couldn't he find peace? He was supposed to be the angel—the one with the surest knowledge that there was some divine plan in place. He believed in a Heaven and Hell, but still wanted to exist perpetually in the realm of the living. Why? His parents would be leaving him soon. And they had to, or else the Maze would collapse on them. *It roams*, a voice whispered in his head. What did Lyrna mean, *'It roams'*?

Jeremy returned to the camp to find a line formed at the door to Lyrna's chambers. Maren gave the okay for the next in line to enter. Frisky gave her a big hug, and then Ren, who would be next. She walked into the room and closed the door gently behind her.

"Jeremy," said Maren. "They wanted a private sorting. I think I'll go privately, too. You're struggling."

"So are you!"

"Jeremy," said Maren in a hushed voice. "There goes Ren. Your parents are next, be strong for them. Here they come."

Jeremy's heart beat wildly.

"I still can't get over Mateo," said Wantoro with a twinkle in his eye. He laughed and embraced his son. "It's okay to cry, Jeremy. I know how you are, and that's okay. You've got a big show ahead of you. You'll see us again."

"Don't go," said Jeremy, pulling him closer. "Please stay."

Raaychila brushed her hand on his arm. "My son. You're not dead yet. I don't suppose you understand how truly ready we are. You've always been my angel."

Jeremy got down on his knees. He threw himself around his mom's waist.

Raaychila kissed him on the forehead. "We love you and we'll see you soon." She freed herself from him, and then held Wantoro's hand. Together they entered Lyrna's chambers.

Maren led Jeremy to a small patch of moss and sat beside him. They watched the rest of the sortings in silence. After the last had gone, Jeremy turned to Maren, his eyes pleading. "Maren, please don't leave me."

"I think I'm ready," she said, her eyes welling up. "I have a lot to be happy about, but I'm scared," she admitted.

"Then you can't be sorted. Scared doesn't cut it."

Maren's lip trembled.

Lyrna's chamber door opened with a squeak and Jeremy hugged Maren close to him.

"I have to go now," said Maren, pushing him away weakly.

Lyrna walked towards them. "Mew." She licked her paw. "Now sort roots, oasis."

Jeremy nodded. "Yes, yes, Maren later then, right?" he said, squeezing her tighter.

Lyrna cocked her head. "No. Maren not dead." Lyrna walked away.

CHAPTER 43

THE ANTICHRIST

Jeremy and Maren embraced, laughed, then cried. They ran over to the oasis and gulped the fluid greedily, fearing its imminent absence.

Lyrna held her paw above the oasis and soon thousands of small threads rose to meet her. "Meow! Meow!"

The walls were shaking. The ceiling broke apart and spirit animals entered the Maze in droves. There were cats of all sizes, racoons, dogs, camels, goats, pigs, and even mysterious species from the Andes; deep-sea dwellers floated by with neon tentacles. The animals packed in tight, pulling chords from the ground, even the doors. Everything, it seemed, was enchanted with soul pieces.

"Much to sort," said Lyrna. "Go, now." Lyrna jumped on Jeremy's lap and licked his cheek. "Now, Apollyon. Have peace." Lyrna jumped off Jeremy's lap and rubbed up against his side. Then she rubbed up against Maren. A final "Meow!" and she ran off with the other spirit animals. The ground rumbled.

Jeremy and Maren only had a few seconds before the ceiling of the oasis room gave way entirely. Jeremy grabbed hold of Maren and shot upward like an energized particle, passing through solid matter. Jeremy cursed at his recklessness and kissed Maren on the forehead. "Good, you're still with me!"

"Jeremy, the key!" Maren pointed across the graveyard. It was bobbing up and down above the gravestones.

Jeremy set Maren down and they ran to the key. Spirit animals swirled all around them, drawing out soul remains and threads from the ground and walls. Jeremy could see the key through the transparent bodies and reached out for it. As he clasped his hands around it, his entire body lit up with a white light. Then the entire ceiling of the Maze crashed down.

Jeremy shot upward through the Earth with one hand on the key and the other wrapped around Maren's waist. They burst into the atmosphere and stared down now as the surface of the Earth collapsed in on itself. After a moment of disbelief, they floated back down to an island of rock on the new landscape, which was flowing with molten-red lava. The sky was indigo, and all around them large rocks were raining down. Jeremy maintained his protective shield. "Maren?"

"Yes?" she managed. The parched, loose Earth beneath them shook.

"Are you hurt?"

"No."

"We need to find a mountain."

Maren nodded.

"I'm going to travel pretty fast... you sure you're okay?"

"I've made it this far. But my belly feels sort of...?"

Jeremy lifted her up so that he could see her belly. He placed his ear to it.

"It feels tight, is all. I can still feel the baby moving."

Jeremy sighed. "Let's give this a try." He fortified his force field and then blasted forward. Everything was a blur, and he stopped after a second. "With me?"

"I'm fine."

"Good," said Jeremy, and he blasted forward again, finding a mountain range that rose high above Earth's molten deadlands. He landed on a cliff that led to an empty cave, and they took shelter in it. When they settled, Jeremy held up the key. "So," he said placing it between them, "am I the Antichrist?"

"No," she said. The wind began to howl outside the cave. Maren shivered.

"Shall we cave draw?" Jeremy bent down and grabbed two stones. He handed one to Maren.

"Sure," she said. Maren lifted her stone and etched a circle into the rock wall. Then she drew a circle around the top, like a crown on a head. She dropped the stone. "Am I the whore of Babylon?"

Jeremy raised his eyebrows and cracked a smile at the idea of Maren doing anything whorish.

She began to recite from memory:

> And the kings of the earth, who have committed fornication and lived deliciously with her, shall bewail her, and lament for her, when they shall see the smoke of her burning....

Jeremy laughed, but was unsure. "No, I only know one ruler who fornicated with you."

"Maybe the Maze was Babylon?"

"No, no," said Jeremy. "And besides, I was groomed to be a ruler, once. But I am no ruler."

"The Whore of Babylon drank freely of wine, and it was the blood of the people."

Jeremy shook his head. "Don't confuse interesting coincidences with an essence—you're pure and true, Maren," he said. "Can you recite more of Revelations?"

"It's the strangest thing," said Maren, "I had the bulk of it memorized. But now my mind's foggy, like I haven't thought about it in years. Time is passing by strangely. When the Haze collapsed I blacked out, and I've never been the same."

Jeremy looked out the mouth of the cave. Smoke was rising from below and getting swept away by the wind. "Well you look pretty pregnant to me. Your arms are too skinny, I wish I could have got you more to eat." Jeremy frowned and looked back at the rock wall.

"It's like a long, illogical dream," said Maren.

They pondered this for a moment.

"Draw," said Jeremy finally. "Sometimes our minds think in images."

Maren accepted the stone and faced the rock wall once more. "I had started to draw a face—I think it was supposed to be me. Then this thing on my head—it looks like the halo."

"Could be a veil." Jeremy scooched next to her. "I'm King, you're Queen." Jeremy scribbled white all over her drawing's body, making it a white block. "We'll just cover you up, all modest-like. No more Babylon lady." He smiled at Maren. "A lovely, pregnant bride. Wanna get married?" Jeremy leaned over and kissed Maren on the cheek.

She smiled. "I'd love to marry you."

"Here's our judge." Jeremy drew a rudimentary figure in a robe on the cave wall. It was holding a book.

Maren bit her lip. "Cajjez Jeremy Chikalto, do you take Maren Nononia to be your lawfully wedded wife, to have and to hold, 'til death do you part?"

"I do." Jeremy smiled and held Maren's hands. "And do you, Gardener of the Maze—Cultivator of the Baby Sprout—Maren Nononia—take Cajjez Jeremy Chikalto as your lawfully wedded husband, to have and to hold, 'til death do you part?"

"I do."

"We may now...?

"—kiss each other." Maren smiled and leaned in. She locked lips with Jeremy and they held tight, savoring the moment. Maren drew back with wide eyes. "Oh," she said, holding her belly.

"Oh?"

"I think I just had a contraction." Maren looked down at her belly and then back at Jeremy.

A great crash came from the heavens and the wind whipped violently through the cave. They ran to the mouth of the cave and looked beyond the edge of the cliff at the wasteland below. Lightning came down from the smoky clouds, and an angel landed on the molten ground. Jeremy pulled Maren close to him. Another bolt, and a second angel appeared. The angels faced each other and held out their palms. A red, swirling mass formed between them. The sky split open and the red mass smoked and groaned as it birthed its way into the dimension.

Maren's breathing became labored. "Does time... unfold... in chronological order... in a dream?"

"Maren, what is that?" Jeremy grabbed hold of Maren. "I'm getting you out of here." He zipped out of the cave with Maren in his arms. He sped to the next mountain over, away from the thing, and they landed softly in a dense thicket of dead bushes.

The air in the distance swirled into a vortex and in its center was the large red mass. The sky lit up and the vortex closed, leaving the large red mass hanging like murder. "How big is that? We must be miles away. What the hell is that," said Jeremy. He sat down beside Maren and clasped her hand. "How are you? Talk to me."

Maren winced and writhed in pain.

"Maren, do you need me to do something?"

A few seconds later, and Maren sat upright. "The contractions are getting stronger. I'm fine now. I can't talk through them. I need you to be ready to get this baby."

"But that thing...?' Jeremy looked back and saw the red mass swoop across the deadlands.

"Jeremy! You have to get this baby. Here comes another contraction." Maren started to breath heavily out of her mouth.

Jeremy looked down the mountain and could see the great beast rising up. It was a red dragon the size of a mountain with seven necks and seven heads, each having ten horns, fast approaching their mountain. Everywhere it went the skies rained blood, and the smell of iron was nauseating. Smoke poured from every pore of its lizard body. Jeremy grabbed Maren and tore through space to another mountain. Maren was screaming. He veered right and flew to the peak. "I'm sorry! Maren, listen to me—can you birth this baby by yourself? It's coming back." Jeremy nibbled at his fingernails. "Can you do this? I have to lead it away from you. Can you do this?!"

"Yes, I think—aaah!" Maren curled up in the fetal position. "I'll be okay. Just thinking about... the new city, prepared like a bride...." She screamed.

Jeremy kissed her forehead. It was all he could do. The Antichrist was coming towards them like a hurricane, and it began to drizzle blood all around them. Jeremy flashed through the air, towards one of the heads, which was the size of a small town. He flew towards the snake pupil, and discharged a bolt of lightning into the black mass. The dragon didn't even blink. Then all seven heads roared and great waves of thunder pulverized the air. Jeremy's head split in unimaginable pain, and his body was tossed aside like a rag doll. He healed quickly. *Maren.*

Jeremy dashed back to her, and she was still laying on her back taking in huge gulps of air. "Are you okay?"

"I survived that noise, if that's what you mean. Aaah..." She winced in pain. She managed to point her finger behind Jeremy, and he spun around to see the largest of the seven heads thundering towards them. It opened its great mouth like a whale, and the head of a man emerged from the throat on a long, scaly neck. The head glowed a soft yellow and his mouth was open in an "O." His eyes were wide and white with no pupils. The neck grew longer and longer as the head careened towards the mountain peak.

"I can't do this by myself," Jeremy whispered and he closed his eyes and lifted his hands, willing his demons forward. They came forth in a black storm and swarmed all over the extended neck, attaching themselves like leeches on a snake, and the head drew back, back inside the dragon's mouth, and the demons went with it, and disappeared into the black hole. The blood-rain stopped.

Jeremy flashed to the far side of the dragon, away from Maren. He unleashed a storm of lightning bolts along the red dragon's mountain of a back, then concentrated them all on a single spot, and finally punctured a scale. Foul red blood sprayed from the scale, but the dragon ignored him. Jeremy jumped into the wound, wading in the rancid flesh, and began to burn it with a white fire, but the mountain didn't flinch. The head had again emerged from the dragon's throat, and the demons were gone. It extended towards Maren.

Jeremy flashed to Maren and found her hiding behind a boulder. Her body was feverish and Jeremy shook her. Time was slowing down and speeding up, going backwards and forwards. The sky rained moon rocks, blood and hail, and lightning flashed. Jeremy made his energy around Maren into an impenetrable diamond. The crib of the Earth rocked violently. Maren's eyes were wide and she spoke these words:

"And the temple of God was opened in heaven, and there was seen in his temple the ark of his testament ... There appeared a great wonder in heaven; a woman clothed with the sun, and the moon under her feet, and upon her head a crown of twelve stars: And she being with child cried, travailing in birth, and pained to be delivered."

Jeremy gripped her by the shoulders. "It's coming again, Maren!"
She continued,

"A huge red dragon, with seven heads and ten horns... The dragon stood before   the   woman about to give birth, to devour her child when she gave birth...."

Maren's breathing became labored.
"But that doesn't happen, right?!" Jeremy turned to see that the head had slithered over to join them, through Jeremy's shield, and was glowing a soft yellow. The white eyes were empty, but the mouth grinned as it drew closer to Maren, ignoring Jeremy.
Jeremy lunged forward to the face and pushed against it with all his might. The faced laughed and Jeremy's heels broke the stone beneath him as it pushed him back. Jeremy reached out with his will and felt his demons inside the dragon. Every demon raged inside the beast, and the face frowned. Seven massive heads now bore down on Jeremy,

who was ant-like below them. He drew his energy tighter and harder around Maren, him, and the head, hard like the point in the beginning of the universe, the first diamond. The dragon heads blasted a primordial fire at his shield, but could not breach Jeremy's diamond. The mouth on the face made an 'O' in surprise.

Jeremy blinked, and in that second, a memory came forward. He was back in the hellscape and his demons' mouths were opened like an 'O.' A rush of sludge filled Jeremy's mouth and he knew the key to escaping death. Jeremy opened his eyes, reached into the Antichrist's mouth, and ripped the snake tongue from its base. The Beast reeled and rolled its eyes back, then opened up its throat to retch. Jeremy grabbed his key from his pocket and pushed his fist right into the face's mouth. He guided the key down the long throat on a thread of light. The face writhed and twisted, and Jeremy pushed the thread further in like a feeding tube. Maren shrieked behind him—and the world coalesced into a blind rage. Jeremy's key reached the pit of the dragon's stomach—the bottom of the red mountain, which began to warble and disintegrated into a river of flesh and blood like a volcano. Jeremy released the head, and blasted it into the river.

Jeremy turned to Maren, and they both wept.

Jeremy reached down and cradled the two babies, a boy and a girl. "Twins," he cried.

A great whiteness flooded their vision. Time hung like a dew drop, full of potential, in the early morning hours. Jeremy smiled across a meadow at Maren, as their children crawled after a ball on the grass. Now Mateo hugged the girl in his arms, and he pointed to a picture in a book. Jeremy held the back of his son along the bike path; he released him and cheered as his boy cycled into a great new world.

Let the author know what you think! Please share your thoughts on *The Hazy Souls* series online through Amazon, Goodreads, and other social media. Thank you!

Jeremy Chikalto and the Hazy Souls
(Book I of The Hazy Souls)
2011

Jeremy Chikalto and Leviathan Island
(Book II of The Hazy Souls)
2012

Jeremy Chikalto and the Demon Trace
(Book III of The Hazy Souls)
2014

Visit our website at
www.viralcat.com
www.tsdebrosse.blogspot.com

www.ingramcontent.com/pod-product-compliance
Lightning Source LLC
Chambersburg PA
CBHW050027180626
46810CB00002B/613